recon

Naoya Shiga (1883–1971) was Japan's most celebrated practitioner of *shishōsetsu*, or autobiographical fiction, the genre that dominated Japanese literature for much of the twentieth century; during his lifetime he was described as the 'god of prose'.

Ted Goossen has translated or co-translated five works by Haruki Murakami; he is editor of *The Oxford Book of Japanese Short Stories* (which includes his translation of Shiga's story 'Takibi') and co-editor of *Monkey Business* magazine, featuring the best of contemporary Japanese literature.

reconciliation

naoya shiga

translated by
ted goosen

CANONGATE

This translation first published in Great Britain in 2020 as a Canon by
Canongate Books Ltd, 14 High Street, Edinburgh EH1 1TE

First published as *Wakai* in *Kuroshio* (Black Tide) in 1917 and
an expanded edition in 1918

This version published in Japan in 1948 by Shincho Press

canongate.co.uk

1

British Library Cataloguing-in-Publication Data
A catalogue record for this book is available on
request from the British Library

ISBN 978 1 83885 045 6

Typeset in Van Dijck by Palimpsest Book Production Ltd,
Falkirk, Stirlingshire

Printed and bound in Great Britain by Clays Ltd, Elcograf S.p.A.

MIX
Paper from
responsible sources
FSC® C018072
FSC
www.fsc.org

TRANSLATOR'S NOTE

Naoya Shiga (1883–1971) was Japan's most celebrated practitioner of *shishōsetsu*, or autobiographical fiction, the genre that dominated Japanese literature for much of the twentieth century. His works form the record of a man determined to heal himself of the psychic wounds left by his early life. His mother died when he was still quite young, and even before that he was raised by his paternal grandparents as the presumptive heir to the family, whose fortunes his father Naohara, a successful banker and businessman, was assiduously expanding. As a result, Shiga grew up much closer to Rume, his strong-willed and fiercely protective grandmother, and her husband Naomichi – a high-ranking retainer to the Sōma clan, until the Meiji Restoration led to the abolishment of the samurai class in 1874 – than to his frequently absent father. Naomichi had passed away by 1917 when *Reconciliation* was written, but he is still a significant figure in the story, as is Shiga's dead birth mother Gin, on whose death day the climatic event takes place.

Although he claimed that the sole topic of his literature was himself and himself alone, Shiga was nonetheless capable of incorporating highly imaginative material into his literature to convey the essence of his experience, as he did in his one long novel, *A Dark Night's Passing* (1937).

In sharp contrast, *Reconciliation*, written in 1917, is highly factual, at least on the surface. Written in a mere five weeks, immediately after the culmination of the drama it describes, it deals with 'universal' events – the births and deaths of infants, the decline of the aged, the struggle between fathers and sons – in a forthright and unadorned, yet psychologically complex style that has served as a model for generations of Japanese writers. A classic in its own right, *Reconciliation* is charged with an elemental force that renders the distinction between so-called fact and fiction quite irrelevant.

The first thing a reader of Japanese notices when he or she picks up one of Shiga's works is how simple the writing is. The sentences are short, the language concrete – indeed, there is something almost childish about the style, with simple phrases like 'It was good' or 'It was bad' appearing at critical junctures. The focus is very narrow, and dominated by the perceptions of the protagonist. Those perceptions, however, can be quite autonomous, operating outside the protagonist's control. When Junkichi visits the graveyard near the beginning of *Reconciliation*, for example, he does not 'remember' his dead grandfather in the normal way. Rather, he places himself in a situation where the dead man's spirit will spontaneously appear in his mind. Once there, the spirit operates on its own, surprising Junkichi with its lack of animosity towards his father. In such situations, Junkichi plays a passive role. He is not the master of his own perceptions – instead, they control him.

This distinction is devilishly difficult to convey in English translations, although it flows quite naturally in Japanese, where the mechanics of subjectivity operate on different principles. One very basic but crucial word, *ki* (気, or *chi* in

Chinese), for example, functions in standard Japanese as an independent entity: when your *ki* 'sinks' you become depressed, when it goes far away you grow faint, when it fastens on something you notice it, and so on and so forth. Japanese people do not treat *ki* in this analytical way, of course: in daily usage, the numerous phrases that incorporate it work like their English equivalents. Nevertheless, *ki* and associated terms reflect a view of the individual that is far less unitary than what we in the English-speaking world are used to.

Junkichi is an extreme example of this. He is dominated by his *ki*, which lives inside him like another self. It dictates his moods, and chooses the objects that demand his attention. When his *ki* turns inward, Junkichi plunges into a dark and unpleasant frame of mind. Obsessions and compulsions force him this way and that. He tries to escape by reasoning his way out, but finds that reason and willpower are of limited effect. Even something so trivial as being forced to wait for service in a bank triggers his malaise. Yet on those occasions when his *ki* attaches itself to things in the outside world, Junkichi is able to merge with his surroundings to an unusual degree.

Paradoxically, the very part of himself that lies at the root of his self-centredness can, when external events engage it, link him to the outside world.

In *Reconciliation*, three such events stand out: the death of Junkichi's first child, the birth of his second, and the illness of his ageing grandmother. The first is especially memorable, one of the most powerful passages in Japanese literature. Until his child is stricken, we can see Junkichi only as an introspective, self-centred man. Yet during the crisis his gaze, directed by his *ki*, never wavers as one procedure after another is carried out on the tiny body. From this point on, gradually, Junkichi begins to work his way out of his trap – at times, he can even sympathise with his father, although the enmity remains. He takes another big step forward when, in the absence of a doctor or midwife, he is forced to assist with the delivery of his second child, a breach of custom that allows him to witness the other pole of the life–death continuum. Buoyed by the presence of his closest friend 'M' (Saneatsu Mushanokōji, a fellow writer who, with Shiga and others, formed the notable arts journal *Shirakaba* or *White Birch* in 1910), things are finally looking up.

When his grandmother falls ill, Junkichi ignores his father's ban and visits the family home. He is shocked by her weakened condition, described by Shiga in the same unsparing manner as the baby's death. Soon, however, word comes that his father wants him out of the house. This is the scene that Junkichi had imagined leading to violence; yet he is able to withdraw without provoking a confrontation. As he says, 'I was exasperated. I was angry, too. Still, since nothing had happened that I hadn't expected, I was able to keep this exasperation from overwhelming me.' The fact that Junkichi had imagined this scene (which, much to his surprise, ends with the father and son embracing) as part of his writing process comes to his aid when the chips are down.

This underlines one of *Reconciliation*'s most striking features: the close relationship between life and art; in particular, between Junkichi's struggle to write and his feud with his father. Shiga had published almost nothing in the four years following his marriage to a widowed cousin of Mushanokōji's, a union his father had vigorously opposed. In the interim, the eminent novelist Sōseki Natsume, recognising his unusual ability, had offered him the chance to serialise a long work about the feud in the *Asahi* newspaper, which would follow Sōseki's masterpiece *Kokoro*. Time and again Shiga struggled to meet Sōseki's and his own expectations, only to fail. 'Well then,' Sōseki suggested when he realised the seriousness of the problem, 'why not write a novel about being unable to write?'

Reconciliation is indeed a novella about being unable to write, strewn with references to failed or aborted works. With the actual reconciliation, however, Shiga's years-long writer's block came to an end. After completing *Reconciliation* in record time, he went on to compose most of his major works in the decade that followed, including short stories like 'At Kinosaki' (1917) and 'Night Fires' (1920) and his one epic novel, *A Dark Night's Passing* (1937), all of which recount, in one way or another, the struggle to achieve a lasting harmony with nature in its many forms. Shiga was widely regarded as having achieved this goal, a reputation earned, one feels, as much by the style he developed than anything else. To the extent that this style relies on untranslatable words like *ki* and associated terms, it may baffle the English reader on occasion. It is my hope, however, that enough gets through to convey the essence of a great writer's work.

I

This July 31st marked the first anniversary of the death of my eldest child – she had lived just fifty-six days. To pay the ritual visit to her grave, I set off from Abiko on my first trip into Tokyo in some time.

When I arrived at Ueno Station, I telephoned my family home in Azabu. A maid answered, and I had her put Mother on the line.

'How's Grandmother?' I asked Mother.

'Better, but she can't leave the house quite yet, so I went to Aoyama Cemetery by myself this morning,' she answered.

'I see. I'm on my way there now as well.'

We fell silent for a moment.

'Will you just be going to the cemetery today?' Mother asked.

'I plan to call on some friends too,' I replied.

Mother lowered her voice. 'Your father . . . he's . . . home today,' she said hesitantly.

'Well, then I'll stop by some other time,' I said, trying to sound nonchalant. Nevertheless, I could feel myself grimace as we continued our phone conversation.

'Are Sadako and Rumeko doing well?' she inquired after my wife, resting after the birth of our second child, only nine days ago.

'They're fine.'

'Is her milk flowing well?'

'Yes,' I said. 'Well, maybe next time . . .'

'He may be going out. Please try again later.'

I said I would and hung up.

I immediately went out and caught the streetcar for Aoyama. On my way to the cemetery, I stopped and bought some brightly coloured flowers. I phoned Mother back but, as I had expected, Father was still there. Once again, frustration and anger enveloped me.

Today of all days I wanted to see Grandmother. For one thing, I sensed that she wanted to see me.

As our first child was born in a Tokyo hospital, Grandmother had been able to see her every two or three days. This time, though, the baby was born in Abiko, and though Grandmother wanted to make the trip, the heat and her poor health made that impossible. She would be wanting to hear from me about the baby. Why should I sacrifice both her feelings and my own just because Father and I couldn't see eye to eye? It was absurd. Yet there was nothing that either Grandmother or Mother could do to break my father's ban on my visits.

I went first to the graves of my birth mother, who had died when I was a child, and my grandfather. My grandfather's brother and his wife were buried here as well. Fresh flowers filled the vases that sat before the gravestones. Since it was my intention to save all my flowers for the baby, I left them and my hat on the clipped hawthorn hedge and continued on to Grandfather's grave.

Except on special occasions, I don't make the customary bows and so forth when visiting graves, a carryover from the Christian precepts I embraced sixteen or seventeen years ago. By walking back and forth before the grave, however, I can resurrect an image of the person lying beneath with a vividness and immediacy unattainable anywhere else.

In this manner, I paced for a while in front of Grandfather's grave. Before long he came back to life in my mind's eye. I told him that I wanted to see Grandmother that day, and asked for advice. 'Go and see her,' Grandfather replied at once. Though the exchange had taken place in my head, it was unusually clear and natural. In fact, it carried that feeling of objective reality one experiences in dreams – I felt he was really there, alive again. Behind his simple words, I could feel him reaching out to touch his ageing wife. And although I condemned Father in my heart, the Grandfather that same heart had called up wasn't critical of Father in the least.

I moved on to my birth mother's grave. Her image was less clear and lifelike. When I put the same question to her that I had to Grandfather, she hemmed and hawed with the indecision of a timid woman, so I gave up trying to communicate and walked on.

I decided to go and visit Grandmother. I regretted the predicament this would place Mother in. Perhaps the best thing would be to go in through the kitchen and then straight up to Grandmother's room. That would allow me to tell myself that I was not entering Father's house, just visiting Grandmother's room. Still, the mere idea of using the servants' entrance was upsetting. If I chose the family entrance, though, I would have to pass through the living room and by the telephone cubicle. Were Father there, a face-to-face confrontation would be a distinct possibility. Nevertheless, I hated the idea of sneaking in through the kitchen.

I arrived at the grave of Satoko, my firstborn. Here, too, the vases had already been filled with flowers, so I laid mine down in front of the grave. Then I set off for Azabu to see Grandmother.

When I reached the Azabu house, I passed through the gate and went in the front door. Mother was there in the corridor, giving instructions to one of the maids. I could tell she was surprised to see me, but she greeted me as usual. I went straight up to Grandmother's room and found her hunched over between two fans; the one placed in front of her was turned off, but the other cooled her back as she sipped sweetened shaved ice with a spoon.

Grandmother questioned me at length about my wife and the new baby. When the weather got cooler, she said, she would make the trip up to Abiko. Then Mother and several of my younger sisters came in, and a maid brought cakes and iced drinks. After about thirty minutes I left, having accomplished my visit without meeting Father.

II

I was writing a piece for a literary journal that had to be finished by 19 August. Every night at ten o'clock I would set to work on it, but the material was proving hard to handle. At first I called it 'The Daydreamer', then changed it to 'The Dreamer'. It focused on my relationship with Father six years previously, when I was living in the small city of Onomichi on the Inland Sea. I personally disliked Father. This was more than the inescapable tangle of emotion that binds most parents and children, I felt: at the root of our mutual animosity was a basic disharmony. But although I found it relatively easy to talk about these feelings, I found I couldn't express them on paper. I didn't want to use my writing to emotionally purge myself. This was partly out of consideration for him, but I was also afraid that it would poison my work.

My feelings were complicated. Just how complicated I came to realise in the process of trying to set them down. Attempting to face my experiences fairly and squarely only taught me that I lacked the strength to do so. The first draft was an utter failure. I didn't think much of the second, either. Finally, with the deadline just six days away, I realised there was no chance of finishing on time. I would have to write about something else. I turned to the topic I had been planning to use for the October issue, which would allow me to give my imagination free rein. By nature I am a slow writer, but this time words poured from my pen like water bursting through a dam. On 15 August, the piece was finished.

The morning of 16 August, I left the house, completed manuscript in hand. I took it to the post office, then boarded the nine-something train for Tokyo. When I arrived at Ueno Station, I phoned a friend to whom I had written suggesting that we get together when I finished the piece. I was told, though, that this friend had gone off on a day-long excursion to Kamakura. I knew 'Kamakura' meant our friend S's place. I wanted to see S too. Why not go? Yet my body was strangely tired, my spirits sluggish and limp. I decided to telephone the Azabu house instead. Mother was called to the phone. She suggested that I come over right away – Father had taken the youngsters to the family villa in Hakone and wasn't due back until later in the day, so she and Grandmother were there alone. Word had reached me that Grandmother had caught a touch of cold that week. I knew Father, being Father, was likely to have left Hakone early in the morning, which meant he might show up during my visit. Nevertheless, I decided to go.

Grandmother was sitting up in bed. She was well on the way to recovery, and her colour was quite good.

About an hour after my arrival, we heard a hue and cry coming from out front. So they've come home, I thought.

A maid came running down the hall to announce that everyone had arrived. No sooner had she left than in came Takako and Masako, the third- and fourth-youngest of my five younger half-sisters.

'We're back!' They bowed in greeting. Takako looked somewhat startled to see me there.

'You know Father came with us!' she said, gazing at me with a puzzled expression.

'Fine, fine,' I replied.

'What about Yoshiko and Rokuko?' asked Grandmother.

'Rokuko's here too,' Takako said.

'Rokuko!' shouted Masako.

'Whaaaat?' echoed a voice from the entranceway.

'And Yoshiko?' Grandmother repeated.

'Yoshiko's the only one who stayed.'

'Whatever for?'

'Father seemed rather cross when he realised we were all coming back.'

'Why?'

'I'm not sure,' Takako said with a quizzical look. 'I was going to stay. But then I ate too many different things yesterday and got diarrhoea, so I decided to come too.'

We couldn't tell from Takako's story why Yoshiko had stayed behind.

'You should have all come together,' Grandmother said.

In ran Rokuko, the youngest.

'Grandmother, Grandmother. Do you know,

Father just played Go the whole time and I got so bored!' Masako pouted.

'That's right,' Rokuko chimed in. 'He just played Go and we didn't get to go anywhere.'

'Fibber!' shot back Takako. 'Didn't we go to Otome Pass?' She glared at little Rokuko, who just shrugged and stuck out the tip of her tongue in mock apology.

In came Father from the corridor. I gave a slight bow, but as I was in the process of uncrossing my legs to shift to a more formal position, the meaning of this gesture was unclear. Father didn't seem to recognise me at first. We hadn't seen each other in two whole years. (To be more precise, I had seen him once near Tokyo Station, but it was a broad thoroughfare, and my wife, who was accompanying me, hadn't noticed, so I was able to look the other way without making it seem unnatural.) Moreover, since I hadn't bothered to shave recently, my appearance was altered by an inch-long beard. When he did realise who I was, however, he looked highly displeased. I sensed he wanted to walk right out, but instead he greeted Grandmother.

'How are you feeling?' he asked.

'A bit better.'

That was all. A tense moment of silence followed. Normally, I am the type of person who stiffens up in these kinds of situations. This time, however, I found myself unexpectedly calm as I gazed up into Father's face. In the past, when Father scowled at me, I would scowl right back. No matter how I tried to control my expression, my feelings would stubbornly prevent me. And long after the event was over, the unpleasantness the exchange had engendered would linger on, adding to my pain.

Silently, Father turned on his heel and left.

When everyone else was summoned to lunch, mine alone was brought to Grandmother's room.

Shortly afterwards, I left the Azabu house.

My body was terribly weary. I thought I might be ill. I decided to head straight back to Abiko, but the train was not due to leave for a while yet.

I owed some money to a book dealer in Kanda, so I went there first. I had thought chatting with him might be a good way to kill time, but just carrying on a conversation was exhausting.

I rested briefly in Ueno Station's waiting room. Once aboard the train, I started getting drowsy, and before long I had fallen asleep. I awoke when we reached Kitakogane and forced myself to stay awake the rest of the way. (Not too long before, I had slept past my stop.)

Safe harbour at last, I thought with relief as I clambered up the steep path to my home. Our hired man, who had been puttering around near the gate, hurried down to take my bags.

'Is something wrong?' he exclaimed. 'You look awfully pale!'

'Welcome home!' my wife greeted me in the doorway. As the light was behind me, she couldn't see how wretched I looked.

'Welcome home, Papa,' she bubbled a bit too gaily, thrusting the baby out for me to hold. My temper was at the bursting point. I pushed past her into the house and threw myself down on the tatami without a word. Her gay mood punctured, my wife came in and anxiously knelt by my side.

'I'm not feeling very well. I'm completely drained.'

'Shall I rub your back?' she asked. Her mood and mine were like oil and water. I got up silently and made my way to the toilet. Diarrhoea. When I came back out, my wife was still sitting there with a vacant expression on her face. Choosing a spot a bit further away, I sprawled out with my back facing her. She put down the baby and moved over to where I lay. When she tried to massage my back, I pushed her hand away.

'What's wrong?' she asked plaintively.

'Just don't touch me.'

'Why are you so angry?'

'At times like this, living with a pest like you is far worse than being single.'

A moment later she began to cry.

My spite seemed uncontainable; I felt I was on the verge of losing control. Yet what a terrible aggravation it would be if my wife's milk dried up. Our first child had not so much died, I believed, as it had been killed by my own carelessness. This time, I had to take all precautions. I managed to check my tongue before things got out of hand.

That evening we summoned the doctor.

I slept for two days.

III

As soon as I recovered, I set about preparing my promised contribution for the October issue. I decided to rework 'The Dreamer'.

Whenever I turned to write about my own life, I had to fight the temptation to indiscriminately record everything. So many events could be recalled, and I felt compelled to list every one. Yet, though each had its importance in the overall scheme of things, there was no way to stitch them together effectively. If I tried, gaps appeared in my writing, and I grew unhappy. Thus I had to struggle to learn to edit out things I really wanted to include.

This problem was especially acute when I tried to write about my conflict with Father. There were just too many incidents.

Moreover, as I have mentioned, I was hampered by my resolve not to use my work to purge my resentment of Father. The grudge I bore him lived within me like another self. Yet it did not fill me, for beside it dwelt still another self that was deeply sympathetic. 'Come what may, I'll never waste another tear on that damned son of mine,' Father had vowed some eleven years earlier. I shuddered to recall the way I'd acted up to then. How many parents are subjected to such treatment by their children? I couldn't bear the thought of having a child of my own behave in similar fashion. When I heard of Father's vow, I felt he hadn't been unreasonable. And I felt alone.

Now, however, Father's open displeasure with me had a different cause. It had been spring, the year before last, when Father had come with my oldest sister to visit me in Kyoto. His aim was to soften the hard feelings left by our earlier quarrels. When I received his telegram reading 'ARRIVING TODAY', my first thought was to set off for Tokyo immediately, making it look as though we'd accidentally passed each other on the train. I didn't enjoy upsetting Father. Yet meeting him would be even worse. I couldn't stand the thought of sitting there chatting away as though nothing were wrong, with my real feelings packed away. I might deceive myself, perhaps even deceive the others, but where would it lead? What we would be left with would be even worse than our original misunderstanding. It would amount to the piling of deceit on top of discord. There wasn't a shred of hope that a true reconciliation might result. Perhaps Father would guess that the timing of my departure wasn't accidental. More likely, though, he would be left in doubt. I made up my mind to leave for Tokyo. At the time, my wife was suffering from the onset of a debilitating nervous condition. Even had she been in perfect health, however, it would have been a terrible burden to have to entertain, after a mere three months of wedlock, unfamiliar relatives in her husband's absence. Moreover, not only were her nerves a concern, our marriage itself had been the most recent bone of contention in my father's and my ongoing feud. When she discovered I was leaving, she broke down in tears. My temper snapped. I stormed out of the house.

Once outside, I began to feel sorry for my wife. She really was being asked to carry too great a load. I turned back home before reaching the streetcar stop.

I decided to write Father a letter. With all due politeness, I told him how I felt in plain and honest terms and explained that I didn't want to see him. Still, I did hope that he would allow me to see my sister. Even as I wrote, though, I had a premonition that he would turn down this last request.

Their train was scheduled to arrive shortly after dark. I sent my wife to the station with the letter. As she was leaving, I told her over and over again that she must personally hand it to Father. She wept.

'If you come back with that letter,' I threatened, 'you can be sure I'll head to Tokyo.'

As soon as she left, I went to visit an Osaka friend of mine at the inn where he was staying.

It was around ten o'clock when I returned home to Kinugasamura. Both my wife and sister were there, along with a cousin of mine who had dropped by in my absence. Everyone looked surprisingly cheerful. My spirits rose as well to see my sister again after so long. Nevertheless, I wasted no time questioning my wife about the letter. She'd had no chance to give it to him at the station, she said, and although they had all had dinner together at Father's inn, an appropriate occasion hadn't presented itself. After returning home in a rickshaw with my sister, they'd discussed the whole matter with my cousin, a joint decision had been reached, and moments ago the rickshaw man had finally gone off to deliver the letter to Father. It was Father's plan, she continued, to take us all on a sightseeing tour of Nara and Osaka. I pictured Father alone in his room at the inn, brooding over my letter. It upset me. But, I thought, there is nothing to be done.

Early the following morning, the four of us set off to walk the path at the foot of Higashiyama in eastern Kyoto that winds south from Ginkakuji, the Temple of the Silver Pavilion, to Sanjūsangendō Temple. The next day we spent in Arashiyama in the west of the city. In the evening we stopped for dinner at a small cafe in downtown Shijō, and I had my sister telephone Father at his lodgings. He was furious, ordering her to return to the inn at once. We said our farewells; then my wife, cousin and I headed back home to Kinugasamura. No sooner had we arrived than a rickshaw man appeared with two letters from my sister. The first, written in Father's presence, asked that her bags be sent back with the rickshaw. The second, a hastily pencilled message written out of Father's sight, described how angry he was, how she had been scolded, and how they were abandoning Kyoto for Osaka the next morning.

More than six months passed. During this time, my wife and I moved three times. First we rented a house in the Yukinoshita district of Kamakura, but when my wife's nervous condition grew worse, we left after only a week and journeyed to Mount Akagi in Jōshū, where we stayed for four months. Then we travelled for a bit before settling down in our present home near marshy Lake Teganuma in Abiko, a town north-east of Tokyo. By this time, my wife had almost recovered. Then she became pregnant.

One day, we went into Tokyo to visit my ailing grandmother. I made arrangements for us to stay overnight in the Azabu house, and then went to visit two friends at their inn in Kōjimachi. It was about midnight when I returned to Azabu. Although everyone had gone to bed, Mother and my wife got up when I arrived. Even Grandmother roused herself for a few minutes to talk to me. After a while, I changed into my sleeping kimono and went to bed. Then Mother, who had gone back to her quarters, reappeared at my door.

'I know this isn't easy for you,' she said, 'but please do come and apologise to your father for what happened in Kyoto.'

I was a bit taken aback. When we had first decided to move to Abiko, I had used the occasion to visit Father's room to pay my respects and inform him of our plans. I intended this show of humility to signal that my feelings had changed since Kyoto, and although he was rather incommunicative, I left with the distinct impression that he was willing to let bygones be bygones.

'Is Father in his room?' I asked.

'Yes, he's up and awaiting your arrival.'

I shifted the knot of my sash around to the back and set off to see Father. He was sitting facing the door, his back to his desk.

'I am not opposed to your visiting this house,' he said. 'Indeed it is my pleasure. However, there is something that needs to be straightened out between us first. What do you have to say?'

'I am deeply sorry for what transpired in Kyoto,' I replied. 'My feelings about you have changed considerably since then. Nevertheless, I still don't consider that what I did was wrong.'

'Is that so! Well, in that case I must demand that you cease your visits to this house!'

'Very well!'

I bowed and left. I was already in a rage.

'We're leaving!' I told Mother and Grandmother. 'If you're coming, then come!' I snapped at my wife as I started to get dressed.

'You don't have to leave right away, do you?' Mother cried, grasping my hands as I tried to do up my kimono. 'If you go now, you'll have nowhere to stay. Wait till the morning, please!' she begged, tears streaming down her face.

My wife too began to plead with me in a tearful voice. I pushed her away in anger. She fell down upon the bedding.

'Sadako, you must go with him!' Grandmother exclaimed heatedly from her bed.

Mother gave in.

I waited for my wife to get ready, then we left the Azabu house together.

The late-night streets were deserted. I set out for the inn in Kōjimachi where I'd been until just two hours earlier, my wife silently trailing a step behind.

'If you disapprove of what I'm doing at all, then you're no relation to me!' I burst out. She remained silent.

'If I were the kind of man who meekly gave in to whatever his father said, I'd never have married you!' I went on in a threatening tone.

Everyone at the inn was fast asleep. Finally, a maid heard me knocking and got up to let us in the side entrance.

She showed us to a small room on the second floor.

The following morning my wife complained that the maid was addressing her in a tone of vulgar familiarity.

'She must think that you're a loose woman because I brought you here so late,' I told her. That made her really angry. She said she wouldn't spend another minute in a place like that.

IV

My wife was expecting in June of the following year. There being no midwives in Abiko, we decided to have the baby in Tokyo. At first, we arranged to have her admitted to a private maternity clinic my wife's aunt knew. Then we found out that Father wanted an obstetrician friend of his to look after the delivery. In early June, my wife moved to the Azabu house. Then, when the time drew near, she was taken to my father's friend's clinic, where she soon gave birth safely to a baby girl.

Father paid one visit to the clinic to see this first grandchild of his. Perhaps because he feared bumping into me, he never came a second time. Yet, when mother and child moved back to the Azabu house some three weeks later, word had it that he was looking in on the baby when no one was around. My wife passed this news on to me with great satisfaction, but I could not share in her naive delight, for I was still strangely distrustful of Father.

She and Grandmother also rejoiced when Father offered to foot all the maternity bills. I couldn't share this emotion either. Yet in the end, I let him pay. Though Grandmother told me again and again to go and thank him for this display of goodwill, I always put her off with some vague reply. Finally, I sent my wife to thank him on my behalf.

I knew that everyone was hoping that the baby would be the bond that reconciled Father and me. Indeed, a silent understanding seemed to have been reached that she was to be used for this purpose whenever possible. I, however, wanted to have nothing to do with this plan.

When, one after another, two of our gate-keeper's children came down with dysentery, my wife took the baby home to Abiko ahead of schedule. At twenty-four days, the baby was a bit young for the train ride, which left her over-stimulated and unable to sleep. By the next day, however, she was fine.

Nearly a month passed. Grandmother wrote to us that Father was wanting to see the baby – couldn't we bring her soon? I felt some resistance to the idea of moving the baby. Moreover, my suspicions of Father's motives remained. Did he really want to see the baby, or was he just reluctant to have eighty-one-year-old Grandmother make the trip to Abiko? Father had always hated these visits of hers. He seemed to be haunted by one thought in particular: should she fall gravely ill in Abiko, he, having forbidden me entry into his home, would have no right to enter mine.

(Though I did visit the family home in Azabu on occasion to see Grandmother, I never slept there. Even when my wife spent the night, I would stay at a friend's, or my uncle's, or else go to an inn.)

Before replying to Grandmother's letter, I wrote to the doctor in Tokyo asking if the baby was old enough to be moved by train. He replied that it was inadvisable to move her until after the hundredth day. On my next trip to Tokyo, I telephoned Mother to pass on the doctor's advice, and to suggest that Grandmother come to Abiko instead.

Several days later, Grandmother made the trip, accompanied by my four youngest half-sisters and the children of my uncle from Akasaka. It was decided that everyone would stay two nights and go back to Tokyo on the afternoon of the third day.

When the time to leave came, Grandmother asked once again that we take the baby to show Father. This request struck me as a bit odd, since the doctor had specified that she be moved as little as possible. Perhaps he had meant 'ideally'. After all, he had permitted the baby to be transported to Abiko after only twenty-four days. Yet, although I agreed to go along with Grandmother's plan, I felt a certain reluctance. Later, I discovered that Grandmother hadn't known of the doctor's instructions. Whether Mother had neglected to tell her, or it had just slipped her mind, I never discovered. Either way, the fault did not lie with them. My personal weakness alone was to blame, for I had ignored my instincts and allowed the baby to be taken to Tokyo. Then, too, luck just wasn't on the baby's side. Had I repeated the doctor's instructions to Grandmother as I had to Mother earlier over the telephone, Grandmother surely would have reconsidered. Why did I remain silent? . . . Anyway, it seems silly to belabour the issue now. For such talk cannot alter the turning point of fate.

At Ueno Station, I put Grandmother, my wife, the baby and the younger children into a waiting taxi, then took the two eldest of my sisters to have dinner in the arcade beneath the Murai Bank. I telephoned Azabu from the restaurant. Their car had struck a bicycle, I was told, but they had changed taxis at Tokyo Station and arrived home without further incident.

After dinner, I said goodbye to my sisters and went to visit a friend. Three more friends joined us, and we ended up gambling through the night and on till noon the next day.

That evening, I left my friend's home and went to pay a visit to my uncle in Akasaka. It was awful weather, wet and blustery. But although my uncle and his wife pleaded with me to stay the night, I longed to lay my exhausted body on my own bed. There, I could sleep soundly.

Determined to catch the last train to Abiko, I braved the storm. By the time I reached the electric tram stop, I was totally drenched.

No sooner had I boarded the tram than I realised with horror that we would be crossing the river on the railing-less Nakagawa Bridge. I don't like those bridges under the best of conditions. If the storm blew us off tonight, then that would be that.

I disembarked before we reached the bridge, at Sudachō Station. Large raindrops were ricocheting off the concrete sidewalk. Looking like a drowned rat in the rain, a solitary workman stood before a shop holding aloft a long bamboo pole with a metal hook on the end. With each violent gust of wind, an exposed wire brushed against this hook, sending down a shower of purple sparks.

I had to find shelter from the storm. All the stores in the district were closed, so I continued on to Manseibashi Station, where I bought an evening edition from a newsboy and settled down on a bench to read it. I had no desire to retrace my steps to my uncle's place. Before long, though, any chance of catching the last train to Abiko had disappeared, so I made up my mind, got back on the tram, and returned to my uncle's.

Exhausted though I was, a strange agitation and some hungry fleas kept me awake all night.

About nine the next morning, I sent someone to Azabu with word to my wife that I was still in Tokyo. Mother sent back a message, however, that she had taken the baby back to Abiko that morning.

I followed on the afternoon train.

V

That evening, we had lit the mosquito incense and started dinner when, in the next room, the baby began to cry.

'Those terrible mosquitoes! Let's have Satoko brought in here,' my wife said.

'Ryū! Ryū!' she called our twelve-year-old nursemaid from where she sat.

Ryū didn't answer. I called her name in a loud voice. At that moment, Ryū's shadow appeared behind the sliding door; then, still not answering, she slid it open.

'I think the baby just threw up,' Ryū said.

Taking the baby, my wife laid her down on a pillow and checked her nappy. She started crying again. My wife inspected the nappy's contents closely under the light.

'It looks a bit green. There's some mucus mixed in it,' she said, knitting her brow.

'Well then don't nurse her tonight. And let's take her temperature.'

'I took it just a short while ago and it was normal.'

I felt the baby's forehead; she didn't seem feverish.

My wife put a clean nappy on the baby and took her in her arms. She started crying even harder.

'Now, now! What happened?' my wife exclaimed as she rubbed her own cheek. 'Hello, hello! That's mummy's cheek!' she went on as the baby tried to move its open mouth towards the spot she had rubbed.

Ryū smiled and went back to the maid's room.

But the baby wouldn't stop crying.

'What's wrong, Satoko?' my wife said, anxiety written on her face. 'Doesn't her crying sound a bit strange?' she asked me.

Actually, it did sound different than usual.

'Some water got in her nose when I sponge-bathed her earlier, but that wouldn't cause this, would it?' she said.

'No, I don't think so,' I said. 'We'd better put her to bed. Is the bedding laid out?'

'Not yet.'

'Well, won't you be quick about it?' I snapped. I was growing angry though there was really nothing to be angry about.

I forgot to mention this before, but not only was my head aching from the accumulated lack of sleep; a large yet-unbroken boil on my thigh was throbbing painfully, further worsening my mood. As soon as Tsune, our maid, had spread out the bedding, I changed into my sleeping kimono and got into bed.

My wife walked to and fro on the darkened veranda crooning lullabies to the crying baby. When the baby finally fell asleep, she came in under the mosquito netting and laid her in the small rope hammock.

She massaged my head for a moment, then went out from the net.

After about fifteen minutes, the baby woke up and started crying again. My wife came in from the living room and stood with her head touching the netting looking in.

'If we keep picking her up she'll never stop,' I said in a low voice. 'It's best to leave her alone.'

'Don't you think something's wrong?'

'Go on back. She'll be all right.'

She left quietly. Though the baby's cries weren't violent, they went on and on. My wife came back in.

'Well, I'm going to sleep, too,' she said, starting to get ready.

I was growing a little worried. At first, I silently fought this feeling. Then, losing patience, I got out of bed, took the baby in my arms and, sitting cross-legged, began to jiggle my body to quiet her. Before long she went back to sleep.

My wife draped her summer kimono over a bamboo hanger, tidied up a bit, then went to pray in front of our family altar (we called it 'the Gohonzonsama') before finally coming under the mosquito net. All the while, neither of us uttered a sound for fear of waking the baby. Then I noticed that the baby's colour was bad. Something's happened, I thought. Just at that moment the baby woke up crying again. I picked her up and tried pressing her face to my cheek. It was cold to the touch. Her lips had a purplish tinge.

'Send the servants to get the doctor!' I ordered my wife. 'One alone might be afraid – you'd better have them both go.'

She left the mosquito net and hurried out into the kitchen.

'Right away, all right? You've got to hurry! Satoko looks a bit strange,' I could hear her telling Ryū and Tsune.

The baby's cries were exceedingly queer now – 'Agh-ha, agh-ha.'

'Go as you are – you must hurry!' I shouted.

My wife came back under the mosquito net.

'Shall I nurse her?' she asked me.

'Give it a try.'

I passed her the baby, but she was past the point of wanting to suckle. Her colour seemed to be worsening before our eyes. My wife was frantic. As if scolding her, she called the baby's name in a rough voice, and heedlessly pressed the small purple lips to her nipple.

I took the baby from her arms. Standing up, I grasped her feet and dangled her upside-down. This didn't work at all. Instead, the baby's complexion took on the colour of dirt.

'I'd better take her myself,' I said to my wife. Still cradling the baby, I left the mosquito net and strode out the unlocked kitchen entrance in my bare feet.

'Aah, aah,' my wife gasped in her despair, and clutched my arm that held the baby.

'What should I do?' she asked.

'Don't follow me!'

'But I can't stand it here alone,' she said, shaking her head in refusal.

'Then go stay at Y's house.'

I hurried out the gate and down to the dark road. It had been raining, and the mud was up to my ankles. The farming family who lived next door were still up.

'Fetch me a lantern – please hurry!' I shouted to them as I passed by their house. Yet I never broke stride. Now I could see the light from Tsune and Ryū's lantern far ahead. I rushed on as fast as I could without jostling the baby too roughly.

'Tsune, come with me to the doctor's. Ryū, you take your mistress to Y's house,' I ordered when I caught up with them. The pale figure of my wife was faintly discernible some forty or fifty yards back down the road. 'Go to Y's place with Ryū!' I shouted at her. 'Don't come this way!'

My sleeping kimono was mud-soaked to the knee and had wrapped itself about my legs, but I hurried on, heedless.

The baby's cries were incessant but weak. She seemed somehow lighter than usual. Her muscles were completely slack. It felt as though I were carrying a dead rabbit.

'Satoko, Satoko,' I called her name from time to time.

We reached the little house of the village headman, which lay at the foot of a small slope outside of town.

'We can see the road now – you run on ahead,' I told Tsune. She quickened her step a bit but made no effort to run. I got a bit angry.

'Why aren't you running?' I said.

'I can't,' she answered. Then I remembered – Tsune had been crippled by a childhood case of rickets. All the same, she hurried on as fast as she could.

The villagers were sitting outside their homes cooling themselves beneath the eaves. We finally reached the doctor's house, only to discover that he was visiting a silk factory another half-mile or so further up the road. I had someone sent to fetch him right away – then a little later I asked that a second person be sent.

The baby's face was altogether different than

usual. There was a faint trembling around her mouth.

I noticed my wife and Ryū standing in the dark shadows of the dirt-floored entranceway.

'You must go to Y's,' I told her. 'If your nerves act up again now, our problems will be doubled, won't they? Now go!'

She seemed to be still waiting for the doctor out on the street. After a while, however, she disappeared.

'Satoko, Satoko,' I called to her from time to time.

I sat on the narrow veranda beside the dirt entranceway looking back and forth from the baby to the street.

'Won't you come in?' the doctor's wife asked me.

'My feet are muddy.'

'I can hold the baby,' she said. 'Please go and wash them.' I handed her the baby and went to clean up in the adjoining kitchen area.

When I returned, the baby had been laid on a folded mattress. The doctor's wife pressed her hand to the baby's forehead.

'There doesn't appear to be any fever, does there?' she said.

The doctor hurried in.

I told him the basic story of how the symptoms had developed: our trip to Tokyo two days before, the baby's seemingly perfect health from our return that morning until the evening, and so forth.

The doctor slipped two fingers of each hand behind both sides of the back of the baby's head and lifted it over and over.

I studied his face. He cocked his head to one side. I could find no hope in his expression.

'There's no fever,' he said. 'It may be a case of brain excitation. When I lift the head like this,' he showed me, 'the chin should touch the chest. The convulsions are quite strong,' he said, looking at the baby's hands. Both were tightly clenched. He showed them to me without a word.

Bringing a reflector with a hole in the middle from the next room, the doctor examined the baby's eyes under the light of a candle.

'How are they?' I asked.

'The pupils are dilated.'

'How is her heart?'

He picked up the stethoscope from where he had tossed it earlier and listened to her heartbeat.

'Her heart is still all right,' he said, removing

the instrument from his ears. The doctor lapsed into thought, sucking the ends of his drooping moustache with his lower lip, as was his custom.

'Anyway, let's try giving her a shot of camphor,' he said. Without hesitation, he set about preparing the injection. He swabbed a spot near the infant's tiny breast with a piece of cotton soaked in alcohol; then, pinching up the skin, he slipped the needle, which was over an inch long, in sideways up to the hilt. The baby didn't seem to feel it at all. The doctor withdrew the needle, pressed the spot with his finger, then covered it with a plaster that he'd stuck to the back of his hand.

'Let's try cooling her head,' the doctor said as he put away his instruments. He sent one of his helpers out to buy some ice.

'Let's give her an enema, too,' he said going into the next room. For no particular reason, I got up and followed him.

It seemed to me that the doctor had given up all hope. Even so, I asked him if she could be saved. He was hard put for a reply.

'Her condition is quite grave,' he said after a pause.

I helped him give the enema. Just then, the

servant who'd been sent for ice returned with the news that there was none to be had anywhere in town.

'Did you try Hanzaemon's?' the doctor asked.

'Hanzaemon doesn't have any either.'

'Perhaps the sweetshop in front of the train station does,' I said. 'Let me use that bicycle and I'll go check.'

Our paediatrician must be summoned from Tokyo, I thought. I borrowed pen and paper and composed two telegrams, one to the paediatrician and one to the Azabu house; then I rushed off towards the station on the doctor's bicycle. I had no light and the road was dark. If you don't keep calm, you'll crash, I told myself as I sped along.

The sweetshop had no ice either. They told me that none had been delivered from the other side of the lake because of the storm the day before – there would be no ice anywhere in town. I was at a loss what to do.

The last train for Abiko was scheduled to depart Ueno Station at nine o'clock. My telegram to the paediatrician read: 'BABY CRITICAL. DOCTOR HERE SAYS BRAIN EXCITATION. REQUEST

YOU COME BY CAR.' To this I now added: 'NO ICE HERE', and sent if off from the station.

When I returned to the doctor's house, I found Y had arrived to lend a hand. He had brought his servant-boy, Sanzō, with him. The old woman from the farm next door had come too, as had Ryū, back from having taken my wife to Y's.

'There should be ice in Yamaichi,' the doctor ordered his son. 'Go get some and make it snappy.' At the same time, Y sent Sanzō and the old woman off to the icehouse across the lake.

The baby's dirt-coloured lips were oddly drawn back at the corners and quivered slightly. Her whole body had grown cold. Her lower abdomen was abnormally swollen as well.

Before long the ice arrived. We shaved some for an ice pack to pillow the baby's head. We placed another ice pack on her forehead. We decided to apply hot compresses to her abdomen. Y went around to the foot of the bed and warmed the baby's feet with his hands. Each of us wanted to do all he could. No one, however, had any more good ideas.

The doctor gave another enema. Nothing resembling stool was flushed out; the fluid he injected came out just as it went in. The doctor touched the soiled spot on the baby's nappy.

'There does seem to be a little mucus,' he said, rubbing his fingers together.

I tried rubbing a bit between my fingertips. It felt slimy.

'Couldn't this be meningitis?' I asked.

'No, it's not meningitis,' he replied. 'Her brain has been jolted, that's all.'

'Ryū,' I called our nursemaid, who had been standing in the entranceway watching us. 'You didn't bump the baby's head when you were carrying her, did you?'

'No, I didn't,' she replied without hesitation.

'If she'd bumped her head you would have known,' said the doctor. 'She would have cried bloody murder.'

'Then the train ride was to blame,' I said. I felt conscience-stricken.

'If the jolting on the train were the cause, her symptoms should have shown up a little earlier,' the doctor said.

'Sadako brought the baby back from Tokyo this morning, didn't she?' Y asked.

'Yes,' I replied. 'Apparently the baby was in fine

shape then. She was already asleep when I got home this evening, but they told me she'd been in good spirits all day long.'

I pressed the ice pack to the baby's forehead as I sat beside her bed. To look at her eyes staring into space was unbearable. I covered them with the cloth from under the ice pack. Just cutting off her sight, I felt, might conserve some of her energy.

'Agh-aah – agh-aah,' the baby's cries continued, but her face showed little suffering. Yet watching her all-out struggle to resist the illness was more than I could stand.

'Her stomach may be hurting her,' the doctor said.

Y's aged housekeeper arrived bearing a flat bottle and a note from Y's wife.

'She says mustard plasters might help,' Y said, looking at the message. 'She has a relative whose child was saved that way.'

'Shall we try it?' I said, glancing in the doctor's direction.

'By all means,' he answered.

He poured some mustard powder from the flat bottle into a dish and mixed it with water.

'Tell my wife to let us know right away if she

has any more good ideas,' Y told his housekeeper as he helped the doctor prepare the mustard. 'And she says you don't have to worry about Sadako,' he reassured me.

I thanked him from the bottom of my heart.

We set about applying the mustard plasters. We spread them from her solar plexus down her lower abdomen, on her back and on both legs.

'Well, ten minutes should be sufficient, don't you think?' the doctor said, glancing up at the clock on the wall.

'Is that all?'

'If they're left on too long, the skin will blister and give us problems later.'

I said I didn't mind a few problems; I just wanted her to get the full treatment. Y agreed.

There was now but faint hope that the Tokyo paediatrician would arrive in time.

'Let's say he got the telegram at nine-thirty,' the doctor said, 'then give him thirty minutes to get ready and another hour and a half to make the trip up here.'

'It only takes an hour,' Y said.

'But driving at night takes longer,' I said doubtfully.

'Then it's eleven-thirty at the earliest, isn't it,' the doctor said.

'Mightn't the roads still be flooded from yesterday's storm?' I broke in again.

The doctor gently peeled back the plaster on the baby's abdomen. The red skin beneath clearly marked its outline.

'It's worked,' the doctor said, moving behind the baby. Still on one knee, he raised and lowered her head a few times.

'You see her neck is bending a bit more now,' he said, looking me in the eye. 'We've reduced the convulsions, though there are still a few around the mouth. Her hands open now, too,' he went on, showing me how her fingers could be pulled back from her palms.

Gaining hope, I looked back at Y.

'She looks a little better, doesn't she,' I said.

'Much better than before,' he replied.

'Now if she starts crying "aaah" loud and steady she should recover,' the doctor said.

'Really! Then cry, Satoko! Let's hear you really cry!' I exclaimed.

'We'd better take off the stomach plasters,' said the doctor, 'it's been fifteen minutes already.'

'I guess you're right,' I agreed, although I really felt like leaving them on a little while longer.

The doctor peeled off a plaster from near her solar plexus.

The skin beneath was a bright red. The doctor took a hot towel that his wife had prepared for him and scrubbed the mark. I felt as though her skin itself might be stripped off.

'Let's leave the back plasters on a while longer,' he said.

The tension in the room was broken by a brief lull.

The doctor spoke.

'You know, the average baby wouldn't have made it through those convulsions. She fought well.'

I could feel joy welling up within me. Mustering all my strength, I called to her again.

'Come on! You've got to cry louder!'

It was a hot and humid night. We were plagued by mosquitoes feeding upon our feet.

Presently Sanzō and the old neighbour woman returned from the other side of the lake with an ample supply of ice. I sent Sanzō to our house to bring back clean clothes and nappies for the baby, a big room-sized mosquito net, and a kimono for myself.

I noticed that my headache had at some point disappeared and that the boil, which had throbbed painfully all day, was no longer a bother. Only an occasional yawn escaped me.

'Aaah,' the baby's cries were growing a little more frequent. We all rejoiced in this. Still, the doctor warned, they had to be even louder. Once they were coming two or three at a time she would be out of danger.

The doctor examined her eyes again with the reflector. I stood beside him watching.

'How are they?' I asked.

'Much smaller,' he answered.

'She may live!' I said. I could feel my eyes sparkle.

Sanzō came back from my home laden with all kinds of supplies. We replaced dirty things with clean ones wherever possible, then everyone moved in under the mosquito net. When the baby was being changed, the doctor checked her abdomen. It was considerably less swollen than before. Little by little, everything seemed to be returning to normal.

'What a blessing if her heart holds up like this until she recovers!' the doctor said.

The clock struck eleven. Thirty minutes, maybe an hour – just a matter of time now, I thought, until the specialist arrived from Tokyo.

Every so often the baby let out a loud cry. On each occasion, our eyes would meet, but despite our prayers her wails grew no stronger.

'Can't you put more into it!' I said, as if scolding her.

Gradually, the time passed. The baby grew neither better nor worse. We expected the sound of the automobile at any moment. 'This may be him!' someone would cry at the slightest vibration, and we'd all strain our ears to hear the motor.

Over and over again we were deceived by the rumble of a passing freight train.

'It's high time he got here,' I said from time to time, looking up at the clock on the wall.

'This time it's him!' Y cried at one point, going outside to check the road. Midnight came.

We had been there four hours. The baby's eyes had been open the whole time. How pathetic it was to see an infant who had always fallen asleep at the breast – indeed, who slept soundly all night with just a single feeding – struggle against death like this.

'Aaah – aaah – aaah!' For the first time, the baby gave three loud cries in succession. Immediately, I turned to the doctor.

'Yes,' he nodded.

Y rejoiced with me at the news.

'If these continue, she's out of danger,' the doctor said. My eyes filled with tears. I could no longer see the baby's face.

'Shall I send for Sadako?' I consulted Y.

'Call her right away!' he said. The doctor too agreed.

I called Tsune, who'd been sitting on the dirt entranceway's narrow veranda, and sent her to get my wife right away.

VI

Yet in the end the baby could not be saved. The Tokyo paediatrician arrived at last around one o'clock, but though he tried his best, it was all to no avail. As the baby's condition worsened, he gave camphor and salt injections at twenty-minute, then ten-minute intervals. He injected the camphor solution into her chest. By the end, the tiny area was so covered with adhesive bandages that there was nowhere left to insert the needle. Her breath stank of camphor. The saline solution was injected into her thighs. In either case, the baby showed no feeling when the shots were given. Even though she was oblivious to what was happening, however, some powerful force of will inside her was clearly working hard to stave off death. By this point, 'Medical Science' was no longer of any consequence. The question now was merely how long her determined struggle to survive could continue. (The Tokyo doctor himself told us this.) As long as she could hold out, there was still an outside chance.

We decided to flush out her intestines. With the Abiko doctor assisting, we gave her enema after enema. Though her abdomen had returned to normal earlier, it had at some time grown swollen again, and this time no amount of flushing could make it smaller. Her lips too, after regaining much of their colour, were again a muddy brown. They twitched and quivered without cease.

It was about four o'clock. The Tokyo doctor announced that he was taking the hired car still waiting outside for a quick trip back to Tokyo. This upset us a little, though we understood it was his way of telling us that the baby was beyond saving. I had no desire to say anything. Nevertheless, I inquired if another one of his patients was in critical condition. 'No, nothing like that,' he replied. Y and the Abiko doctor were openly disgusted and suggested that he stay a while longer. Finally, we arranged for Y, who had an appointment in Tokyo, to take the car and send back another paediatrician, a friend of this one, to take over. This new paediatrician also happened to be an acquaintance of Y's.

Outside, the morning sky was brightening.

The baby's body was growing colder. Her heart was weakening. We decided to guard against this by applying hot towels. Y's wife, who had been taking great pains to help with Sadako and the baby from early on, sent Sanzō to her home and mine to bring back all the towels he could find.

Sanzō returned with a number of towels, including two big tatami-sized bath towels. The doctor's wife had set cauldrons of water boiling on the stove. First Y's wife, then Tsune and Sanzō, took turns going down the dirt corridor to the kitchen, wringing out a towel in the scalding water, and bringing it back to us. At first, we opened them up to cool a bit before wrapping them around the baby's back, chest and legs. But though we warmed and warmed her, her body remained cold to the touch. She seemed to recover somewhat at first, but this lasted less than twenty minutes. Then her heartbeat began to weaken again. Now eight people were hard at work just trying to keep the baby warm. Even the Tokyo doctor was doing his utmost. I thanked them all in my heart.

Nevertheless, I felt it somehow a pity for the baby that none of her closest kin from Azabu were there. I was not exactly satisfied with myself either.

Though we constantly changed the towels on her back, chest and legs, the baby grew no warmer. By the end, we were frantically wrapping her in towels too hot to hold against our own skin, even for a second. I'd given up all hope by this time and had no inclination to reflect on what future disfigurement might result. I just didn't want to let her die.

Her belly was growing more and more swollen. I felt that if whatever was in there came out, something might change. The Tokyo doctor inserted a narrow rubber tube as far up the baby's rectum as it would go and began giving her an enema.

The baby's strength was steadily ebbing. Nonetheless, she fought on with all she had left.

Leaving the rubber tube set deep in the rectum, the Tokyo doctor unhooked the syringe from it and tried sucking out whatever was in the intestines with his own mouth. What he managed to extract he spat out in a nearby metal washbasin. It didn't amount to much, though. As he was doing this, the baby stopped breathing. A black muddy liquid came bubbling from her nose and mouth. It flowed in a wide stream across her pale cheeks and down towards the nape of her neck. The doctor hurried to wipe it away and started to administer artificial respiration, but this was no more than an attempt to console us.

My wife gave a wild cry and collapsed.

'Be strong, Sadako, be strong!' Y's wife said, lifting her up and clasping her face against her breast as tears rolled down her cheeks.

I wept. I wept as I had when my mother died.

VII

We dressed the baby in her best kimono, which we had brought from our house. Then, giving her to Sanzō's wife to hold, we all left the doctor's house together. The weather was fine and clear. My wife took a new handkerchief and carefully covered the baby's face. The previous night we had hastened along this country road by the light of a lantern; now we walked home down the same road under the brilliant summer morning sun. Sanzō's wife preceded me by about fifty yards or so, carrying the baby. Six or eight yards behind me followed my wife, her face turned towards the ground.

Mother came in response to my telegram of the night before. My wife's parents arrived a bit later, having received our cable announcing the baby's death. Still later T, the husband of one of Father's cousins, came from Azabu.

'What a tragedy,' T said. 'I telephoned your father at the Hakone villa to request instructions as soon as I read your telegram. His orders were to have Satoko buried in the temple-grounds at Abiko.'

My blood began to boil as I listened to him.

'We have no idea how long we'll be living in Abiko,' I said. 'Our intention is to bury her in Tokyo.'

'Oh, I see,' T replied, ending our conversation.

I was upset with everyone at the Azabu house, even Grandmother and Mother. Though last night's telegram had said 'critical', not 'please come', my added request that the doctor be sent by car hinted that they might join him too if they were coming anyway. When I discovered that all Mother and Grandmother had taken the cable to mean was that I had been alarmed by the baby's convulsions, I became even angrier. Not even a simpleton could overlook the word 'critical'. I was particularly furious with Grandmother, who had been so eager to take the baby to Tokyo. Then there was T and his 'request for instructions'. He should know, I thought, if I were really the sort to submit so meekly to Father.

Actually, I'd been feeling quite emotional up to that point. My birth mother, who at her death had been younger than I was now, was buried in Aoyama Cemetery, and for her sake as well as the baby's, I wanted her first grandchild to be lain nearby. I was reluctant, however, to mention this desire to anyone. I didn't want to give the impression that I was asking to have Satoko buried in the family plot. I commissioned T to purchase another plot of a hundred square feet or so at Aoyama, and to go through the procedures and preparations to have her buried there the following day. I told him that, rather than have some unknown priest from god-knows-where perform the rites, I wanted him to ask my uncle's teacher, the abbot of Kamakura's Kenchōji Temple, to bestow her posthumous name and chant the sutras on the same day there in Kamakura.

Our friend SK the artist came from Tokyo. That night he kept the deathwatch with us.

My wife and I placed a number of things inside the coffin – our photograph, her treasured Sashirō dolls, a kimono from her home with her family crest on it.

The next morning, a hired car arrived from Tokyo. It was decided that SK, Y and I would use it to transport the coffin back to the city. In the meantime, it would wait for us at Daikōji Temple in town. To help carry the baby to Daikōji, the carpenter and gardener who sometimes worked for us came dressed in new livery. They shouldered the small coffin on two freshly cut green bamboo poles, then we all set out across the rice-field paths and up the slope. When we passed by the home of some acquaintances of ours, the old lady of the family came out with a great bunch of flowers to see us on our way. We asked her to lay the flowers on the coffin.

Since seventy-five days had not yet passed since childbirth, my wife remained at home.

That morning, I had received a telegram from my uncle requesting that the coffin be taken directly to his home in Akasaka. Father has refused to let it be brought to Azabu, I thought. I felt a deep surge of resentment. My thinking went as follows: had the family not attempted to use the baby to reconcile Father and me, she wouldn't have died. No matter how I agonised over having gone against my feelings to let the baby be carried off to Tokyo, it could never be enough – nothing could be changed now. I just wanted to do everything possible for the dead child. In fact, however, Father had not only barred the coffin from his house, he had forbidden the baby's little aunts and great-grandmother to visit Uncle's. 'No one is going to Akasaka!' he had said. Hearing this made my gorge rise. How could Father have extended his anger with me to the baby like that? Having just watched with unswerving gaze as the baby struggled against, then succumbed to, the unnatural death that had so relentlessly pressed upon her, I found his action repugnant, indeed, unforgivable. It was my unresolved relationship with the Azabu house, I thought, that lay at the root of the matter. I was angry. Yet I could not move to fix the situation for fear of sacrificing my ties with Grandmother. Yes, it was from this dilemma that all else stemmed and I could not resolve it, angry though I was.

It interfered with my work as well. How many times in the last five or six years had I planned a major work based on my discord with Father? Yet every attempt had ended in failure. Though my lack of patience and my stubborn refusal to purge my grudge towards Father through my writing played a role in these failures, the main reason was that my mood would darken whenever I thought of the real-life tragedy publication of my manuscript would bring. It was especially excruciating to imagine the dark shadow it would cast over my relationship with Grandmother. About three years earlier in Matsue, I had tried my best to avoid this tragedy by sketching the following outline for a novel-length work: a melancholy-looking youth visits me (the narrator) at my home. He is serialising a story in the Matsue newspaper. Then he starts sending me the instalments to look over. They concern his feud with his father. Not long afterwards, the newspaper abruptly breaks off the serialisation. The youth comes to visit me again, this time in a highly agitated state. Though he has been publishing the story under an assumed name, his father has found out anyway and has sent someone from Tokyo to pay off the newspaper to quash it. There follows a series of unpleasant incidents between father and son. I described these in the third person. Close to despair, the enraged youth's relations with his father grow more and more foul. The father strictly forbids him from entering the family home. I wrote about these and other unpleasant events that might take place between Father and me to try to prevent them from coming true in reality. I thought if our future course were set down so clearly, we might be able to stop ourselves in time. I planned the final climax to be the foulest tragedy of all. The grandmother would be lying close to death. Determined to let nothing stand between him and his dying grandmother, the overwrought youth would force his way into the family home; a fight, probably a violent one, would ensue, and then either the father would kill the son or the son the father – I wasn't sure which. This was how I originally planned the composition. Yet, just when I was picturing the peak of the final battle, the two suddenly threw themselves into each other's arms and burst into tears. This unexpected development caught me completely by surprise. I wept.

Nevertheless, I did not make a final decision to resolve the 'catastrophe' in this manner. Such things, I felt, could not be planned in advance. Only when I reached that point in my writing would I know for sure. Still, I thought, if it did turn out that way, how wonderful it would be!

I wrote a bit of this novel but never continued it. My subsequent marriage caused the colours of Father's and my discord to deepen once again. Despite this, I still felt that the scene that had once appeared in such a spontaneous and natural way might yet materialise for Father and me. It was not inconceivable that it would come suddenly when our relationship was at its most wretched. Then again, perhaps it wouldn't happen at all. Though I wouldn't know for sure until we reached that point, I sensed that something still dwelt within both of us that could produce such a sudden reversal. I mentioned this to my wife and one of my friends.

VIII

After the baby died, our house suddenly became very lonely. When we took our chairs out to the garden to enjoy the cool night air, the distant cries of forest birds drifted across the lake to us – aagh, aagh. Moments like these were unbearable.

We were sick of Abiko. We talked of moving back to the outskirts of Kyoto at the end of the year.

When Y left on a trip to Korea and China ten days after the baby's funeral, Abiko grew even more lonely. Just then my oldest and dearest friend, M, came with his wife to spend a few days with us. M said a doctor had told him his lungs were diseased. I felt desolated. Yet somehow I sensed that the harmony of his body had been disturbed for a brief spell, no more. I tried encouraging him to live in Abiko but forgot to mention our planned move to Kyoto. My only thought was that this marshy land with its pine forests and moist, relatively warm winters would be good for someone with a respiratory ailment.

M and his wife did find a spot they liked on a pine-forested hill and set about building a new house there, but it was in a neighbouring village, not in Abiko. Then, just when all was settled, M learned that his lung ailment was nothing more than the doctor's faulty diagnosis.

A trip seemed like a good way to help us forget the shock of the baby's death more quickly. We decided to leave on 20 August, following the twenty-first-day death observances and exactly seventy-five days after my wife's delivery.

My painter friend SK had just left on a vacation with his family to Kanbayashi hot springs in Shinshū, so we decided to go there. On the morning of 20 August, my wife and I went to Tokyo, where she visited the baby's grave for the first time. Then I went to see a friend. My wife went on alone to the Azabu house. We agreed to rendezvous at Azabu's Roppongi streetcar stop so that we could go on together from there to Ueno to catch the Shinshū train. But my wife was unusually late. Growing impatient, I started walking in the direction of the Azabu house when I saw her hurrying towards me. Her face was drawn and tired, but her feet moved briskly. I felt peeved, not just because of her tardiness but because I found being barred from the Azabu house so humiliating. I scolded her.

On the streetcar, my wife described how Father had flared up the moment she stepped into his room, demanding to know why the baby's body had been brought back to Tokyo. Grandmother, Mother and my younger sisters had all gone to the Hakone villa earlier in the day. Only my second sister Yoshiko and Father were there. My wife was going through a very emotional period around this time, verging on tears whenever she met anyone. Tears were already falling when she entered Father's room. No doubt she was unconsciously expecting him to say 'I'm sorry about Satoko', or something of the sort. Instead, all of a sudden, he flew into a rage. She was utterly dumbfounded. My wife wept as she told me her story. Filled with fury towards Father, I said something to her in a tone halfway between consolation and anger. I realised the other passengers were staring at us, but my anger was stronger than my sense of shame.

At Ueno we boarded the Kobe-bound night train that would take us to Shinshū. The moment I got on the train I was overcome by the helpless sensation that we were going to crash. I borrowed my wife's stiff kimono sash bustle and crammed it between my head and the wooden seat. In case of a smash, I thought, it might help cushion my head from the hard boards. Though we couldn't sleep because the car was so crowded, otherwise the trip passed without event. When we reached Kanbayashi that night, however, another menace rose to threaten me – earthquakes! Every so often there was a rumbling sound and the earth shook. My patience finally wore out on our third day there. I couldn't fathom how everyone else could be so calm. I kept trying to convince SK we should pack up and move out. He, on the other hand, wanted to stay on and work, for he was about two-thirds finished with a large oil painting. I found lingering even a minute longer nerve-wracking. None of the others, however, could see why we had to pack our many bags that very night, load them, ourselves and SK's child, who was slightly under the weather, into rickshaws, and set off on a twelve- to fourteen-mile journey.

All five of us left Kanbayashi the following day with the great pile of luggage we had brought for a two-month stay, much to the amusement of the innkeeper and maids.

Though the only concrete result from all this was to inconvenience poor SK, at the time I was convinced that those laughing at us were fools to risk their lives by staying on. A short time later, when we had moved to Yamanaka hot springs in Kaga prefecture, we saw in the newspaper that the earth tremors in Kanbayashi had grown so severe after our departure that officials had been sent to Mount Kasahōshi to investigate.

After about a month, we parted company with SK and his family and went to Kyoto. We toured Nara, Hōryūji Temple and Ishiyama on foot before returning to Abiko early in October. Three or four carpenters from Tokyo were hard at work building M's new house.

When we'd set out on our trip, what my wife had feared most was seeing a baby about the age of our dead child. I myself was quite unmoved by such a prospect. Sometimes when we were out together she would slip away without telling me. I would usually find someone there was holding a baby. As time passed, however, her fear began to fade.

One day in November, the eldest of my sisters, who lived in Kamakura with her naval-officer husband, gave birth. It was a girl. Grandmother sent word to us that she was taking my younger sisters to see the baby on Sunday – wouldn't we like to come? Despite some misgivings, my wife wanted to go along.

Early on Sunday morning, we left Abiko and went to join Grandmother's party at Shimbashi Station. Our first stop in Kamakura was my uncle's house. For over ten years he had been engaged in Zen meditation at Kamakura's Kenchōji Temple, but eye problems had forced him to move to a rented house in Akasaka so that he could make regular trips to receive treatment. He had lived there for over a year, but in September his eyesight had finally improved, and he had returned to Kamakura.

Both my sister and her baby were in good shape. Before my own was born, all babies had looked the same to me, but this one was quite unlike my dead child. Actually, it did remind me of Satoko a little bit, but not all that much. This sister of mine had been born on New Year when I was fifteen. I talked about that night. I had been waiting in the sitting room, full of anticipation since I had no brothers or sisters, when the grandmother of my Kamakura uncle came in holding the baby. It was a strange-looking thing, bright red with an absurdly long head. Now that baby had given birth to this one.

My youngest sister, Rokuko, put her face near the baby and sniffed.

'Satoko smelled good when she died,' she blurted out. The inside of Satoko's casket had been sprinkled with perfume – this is what she had remembered. Startled, my wife gave her a poke in the back.

A moment later, my wife abruptly got to her feet and rushed out to the front hall. I followed shortly afterwards to see how she was.

'Tell everyone I'm sorry. I don't know what's come over me,' she said through her tears, repeating 'I'm sorry' over and over again. 'How nice these things don't bother you,' she added sarcastically in the midst of her apologies.

I had someone take her back to my uncle's right away. I followed a little later with Grandmother and her youthful entourage.

As soon as she saw me, my wife took me aside.

'What should I do?' she asked. 'I came determined not to cry. It's so unfair to all of you . . .'

'It can't be helped. Just let it be. No one took it the wrong way,' I said, but she kept on anyway. I gave up and went back to talk to Grandmother.

Her back rounded, Grandmother sat hunched over her knees smoking her pipe. A red-eyed Sadako came back out to join us. She sat down in front of Grandmother, then suddenly threw herself down in a deep bow.

'Grandmother,' she said, her voice shaking. 'Please forgive me.'

Still bent over, Grandmother sat there in silence, the pipe stem clenched between her teeth. Her lips were trembling.

At that moment, I felt ashamed for having hated Grandmother so when the baby died.

IX

Shortly after the Kamakura trip, we learned my wife was pregnant again. I felt it was still too soon. Certainly we could have another child, but a bit more time should pass first. My wife, however, was elated. Grandmother was overjoyed as well. Since I'd held Grandmother partly to blame for the baby's death, I was happy for her sake it had come so soon.

When M moved into his new home in the next village, Abiko grew more lively. Since I'd been living outside Tokyo for five or six years, this was our first chance to see each other regularly in a long while. As the days and months passed, I could feel my old love for M revive, this time in a new, expanded form. This reawakening was a happy event for me, one that influenced my whole being for the better. M really had a remarkable power to draw the best out of whomever he was with. He also relished direct heart-to-heart communication. I was always able to count on him. And so my days came to be filled with a feeling at once relaxed and alert.

Four years earlier in Matsue, finding myself unable to continue the novel-length work I mentioned earlier, I had resolved to lay down my pen for a while. Anyone whose state of mind was so bad, whose heart so wretchedly impoverished as mine, I thought, should never have committed himself to setting down his innermost feelings in the first place. Since then, I had scarcely written anything. The few attempts I did make quickly ended in failure. Though I didn't want to give up writing, I did find it quite disturbing that I could feel none of the excitement I had six or seven years before.

It was February. A close friend who had also had to give up writing temporarily (in his case, for reasons of health) and I decided to meet on Saturdays to put together an informal literary journal to circulate among our friends. Our launching of this journal was meant half in jest.

Still, we thought, what started as a joke might lead to something more serious. Unchastened by my prior failure, I started writing another long work to serialise there. I wrote instalments for the first three issues, broke it off to publish a short story in the next issue, then added another story in the next one. At that point, however, a blunt-spoken doctor gave my friend some distressing news about his condition. Our little journal naturally fizzled out. Nevertheless, I wrote one more short piece from sheer force of habit. I showed it to no one. I continued to scribble for one or two nights before each Saturday, but had no confidence and didn't feel like publishing any of it.

Just about that time, someone from a certain publishing house came to ask my permission to publish one of my earlier works in a series they were putting out. They had originally broached this idea with M when soliciting one of his stories, but he had indicated I would refuse and then never mentioned it to me. When I heard this from M's wife, my reaction was to let them publish it. This could be the spark, I thought, which would stimulate me to produce new work. I felt capable of writing something.

One day I showed M the two short stories I had written for the journal. One he called 'solidly written'. The second struck him as conveying a 'spirit of quiet melancholy'. He encouraged me to publish them. As we walked back to his home across the country roads, he offered some perceptive and sympathetic comments about my writing. I decided to include one of my stories in the next issue of *White Birch*.

The timing was probably accidental, but just two or three days later a magazine company representative came to urge me to write something for them. I agreed to let them publish another of my short stories the month after next. Soon afterwards, I received a request from yet another magazine. I still had one unpublished story left, so I decided to rewrite it for them. It was based on a scene that had come to me the previous summer when my wife was in a Tokyo hospital having our baby.

There was a husband, so this fantasy went, who although honest did not lead what you could call an irreproachable life. For one reason or another, his wife was absent from home for some time. While she was gone, their maid became pregnant.

The husband, however, was not the father. Though he could maintain his innocence in the matter with a clear conscience, he knew he was the kind of man who would be suspected anyway. Finally, when the maid's condition had become unmistakable, he went to his wife. 'The baby's not mine,' he told her. 'I see,' she answered just like that, trusting him on the spot. This was all I wished to write. Both husband and wife were wise. The tragedy failed to materialise. I intended the story to show how such potential tragedies could be averted. As my own life improved and my state of mind grew more harmonious, I found it increasingly upsetting that so much unhappiness was caused by those whose stupidity led them to doubt things that they should have believed unquestioningly. Needless to say, I wasn't thinking of others' foolishness alone.

The story, however, turned out to be a failure. Had I not promised to deliver it on a fixed date, I might have been able to rewrite it so as to better express the way I felt. As it was, I sent it off on schedule in its unsatisfactory state.

Not long afterwards, a certain newspaper asked for about ten pages of my diary or any other random thoughts and impressions I might have jotted down. What I sent them instead was a piece barely two and a half pages long entitled 'A Son and His Parents'. I enclosed a letter with it explaining that, since it wasn't what they'd requested, I wouldn't be offended if it was rejected, although I wanted it mailed back to me. This piece was actually taken from a two-hundred-page manuscript authored by a young post office employee I had once known – I had just arbitrarily chosen the excerpt and fixed up his style a bit. I added a simple acknowledgment to this effect.

This particular young man had become involved with a beautiful girl who worked on the post office switchboard. Their affair was discovered by the postmaster, who admonished them for their 'shameless and ugly behaviour' and promptly fired them both. Shortly before that, however, the youth had divulged all to his parents and asked their permission to marry the girl. It was his account of this conversation that I excerpted for the newspaper. In it, the father readily gave his consent to the marriage, causing the mother to weep for joy. What I liked about this scene was its direct opposition to my own family situation, where things that could be settled easily and without conflict were twisted into painful and unnecessary tragedies. I chose the title 'A Son and His Parents' to contrast my relationship with Father to that of this father and son, though I realised that only that handful of people close to me who knew of the three or four times Father and I had clashed over my marriage would understand the connection.

I could feel my own state of mind growing steadily better. Was it really all right to feel this happy? I wondered. It was, to be sure, an advance over my prior disharmony. Still, I thought, one couldn't write about the good fortune of a lucky hero forever.

Bit by bit, this newfound harmony began to work on my relationship with Father. On occasion, however, my mood would be disturbed. Once, for example, when my wife and I were in Tokyo together, we telephoned Azabu to see how Grandmother was doing. Mother answered and suggested that we come right over – Father had just left. We took the streetcar to Azabu. Just as we arrived, little Takako, who had been standing there waiting for us, came running out. 'Father's back!' she whispered to us. Having already entered the front gate, we had to turn right around and go back without seeing anyone. Not surprisingly, such moments disturbed my peace of mind. Still, when I heard rumours of how difficult and short-tempered Father could be with my sisters, I couldn't help thinking that our discord was to blame, and that the happy balance I'd gained was mine alone. On these occasions I sympathised deeply with my ageing father for his unfortunate state of mind.

X

The day of the birth drew steadily nearer. We decided to have the baby in Abiko this time. It was far better for both mother and child, I felt, to take every precaution there in the country rather than risk moving the two of them home by train from a Tokyo hospital after three or four weeks. Still, the worry that there might be unexpected complications kept passing through my mind. Perhaps the death of our first child had made me a bit too timid. It was good to be cautious. Too much timidity, however, could conversely lead one to take foolish risks. I resolved to rid myself of my uneasiness.

For our midwife, we decided to hire the same one from the year before. For our doctor, we decided on the Abiko doctor. As nurse, we chose the older woman who lodged at the midwife's home whose obstetrics' training qualified her to deliver babies.

The nurse came on 13 July.

A week passed without any sign that the birth was imminent. I decided that when the time came, I would go stay at Y's until it was all over.

One day, on a hunch, the midwife came from Tokyo. Her hunch was wrong, however, so she went back early the next morning.

A friend of about two years named K paid us a rare visit during this time. K was a recent father. He said that a single sneeze from the baby was enough to give him the jitters.

K's child had been born in a Tokyo hospital. When they phoned his home to tell him that the birth was due any minute, he was thrown into such a strange state of nervousness and uncertainty that he could only fidget there by himself until news of the safe delivery came. He rushed to the hospital to find the newborn infant already lying on a small quilt next to his wife. 'Ho-ow about that!' was his first thought, he told us. There was something in K's 'Ho-ow about that!' that really made us laugh.

K had picked up a smattering of knowledge about child-rearing, so he and the nurse had a lot to talk about.

A little while later, my wife mentioned that her belly was acting a bit queer. After getting a few more details from her, the nurse asked K, 'How does it look to you at this stage?'

'Perhaps tomorrow afternoon around two o'clock,' he answered. 'That's the feeling I get.' When we questioned him further, we found out that his own child had been born about two in the afternoon.

K returned to Tokyo shortly afterwards. I accompanied him as far as the train station. When we parted, he agreed to phone Azabu on his arrival to give them the news. My wife's condition, however, quickly returned to normal.

It was the evening of the twenty-third. We had taken our chairs out to the garden to enjoy the cool breeze blowing across the lake when my wife said, 'I think the contractions are starting!' Even if the midwife were contacted immediately, she wouldn't have time to catch the last train. If we were going to hire a car for her, the nurse said, we might as well wait a little longer and see how things went. 'I doubt it will be before tomorrow morning, maybe even noon,' she predicted.

We decided to go to bed. As my wife was in no great pain, we all fell asleep leaving things as they stood. At about one-thirty, however, she went into labour. Roused from my sleep by the sound of her voice, I got up and woke the nurse. Next I woke Tsune and Hisa and set them to work boiling water. Then I lit a paper lantern and set off for the train station, our dog Teru at my heels.

Since after-hours telegrams weren't handled in Abiko, I could only rely on the good offices of the station officials to bend the regulations and make a telephone call for me on their line. After our first baby's death the year before, the assistant stationmaster had kindly offered me the use of their phone in case of emergencies. He was no longer there, having been transferred, so I asked his successor. Although happy to help, he had an unexpectedly hard time getting through to the Ueno end. Even when, at last, they seemed to have come on the line, he still couldn't get my message across. At this point, the freight train from Tokyo pulled in, and he had to run out to the platform to hand over the proper papers. His place was taken by the familiar face of another official, and after much difficulty he finally managed to put my call through.

I rushed home.

'Not yet, it's not time for that yet!' the nurse was telling my wife as she carried on all by herself.

I'd planned the birth to take place in our eight-mat Japanese-style room. The nurse was determined it was to be in the adjoining six-mat room. Though she was a kind and good-natured woman, she was also stubborn, and refused to do as I said. I got angry and dragged the bedding from where she had already arranged it to where I wanted it to go.

It was still pitch-black outside. There was no way that I could flee to Y's house when he was still fast asleep.

'If the time comes and you need me, I'll be in the garden,' I said to the nurse.

There must be some sort of rationale, I felt, for the age-old custom that a husband shouldn't watch his wife give birth. It certainly wouldn't be good if his presence made her worry about how unattractive her face or her posture might look; bearing the baby safely should be her only concern. For my part, I didn't think seeing my wife in such an unseemly state was a very good idea. Having to stare at her suffering didn't appeal to me either.

From time to time my wife's contractions would come on, then ease off again. The periods of rest in between the contractions, however, were growing steadily shorter. I sent Hisa to Sanzō's house to tell him to go get the Abiko doctor.

Night was giving way to day. We could hear the flurry of wings as the doves in the eaves outside the entranceway took to the air.

My wife's contractions were becoming more and more intense. I was unusually on edge, and kept walking in and out of her room, though there was nothing for me to do there in the house. There seemed to be no way I could lend a hand. Yet I didn't feel like sitting alone out in the garden after having put the young maids so hard to work. What was there for me to do? There was no particular job for me.

'Sir! Sir!' the nurse called. I went in.

'Please hold your wife's shoulders down!'

I went directly to the head of the bed and pressed my big hands down firmly on both her shoulders. With her own hands clasped tightly on her breast, she was pushing with all the strength in her body. Her pale face was twisted with exertion, and she ground and ground away at the folded piece of gauze that had been placed between her eyeteeth. Her face was unusually beautiful. It conveyed a sense of total commitment.

'We've got a real race here! Who's going to come in first – the baby, the midwife, or the doctor?' The nurse chattered away, trying to look calm. Yet I could see that she was tense.

My wife held her breath and squeezed her eyes tight shut. I forced more strength into my cramped arms.

'The baby's won! The baby's won!'

A fountain of water spurted a foot in the air. Simultaneously, the dark head of the baby emerged. Then, like a stream bursting through a dam, its little body flowed out between its mother's parted knees. Immediately, it let out a loud first cry. I was overcome with emotion. I thought I was going to weep. Paying no heed to the nurse's presence, I kissed my wife on her pale forehead.

'Bravo for the baby! Bravo for the baby!' the nurse said as, face beaded in sweat, she quickly cleaned up. She rose and went out, leaving the baby right where it had landed. It was howling even more vigorously and kicking its mother's thighs with its small feet.

Breathing deeply, my wife raised her eyes to mine, and a weak but peaceful smile floated to her lips.

'Fine, fine,' I nodded, close to tears. I felt that I wanted to give thanks to something. My heart clearly required an object on which to bestow its gratitude.

The newborn infant called up no special parental emotion in me. I felt no urge to go over to where it lay to take a closer look. Nor was I in any hurry to find out whether it was a boy or a girl. I was only aware of the lingering feeling of joy and tearful excitement that had filled my breast at the time of the birth.

Childbirth – not a thing about it had been ugly. One reason was that it had been completely natural. There was not a hairsbreadth of unsightliness in my wife's face or the posture of her body. All had been beautiful.

Afterwards, too, everything went smoothly. The Abiko doctor came, followed by the Tokyo midwife; then, a little later, Mother arrived from Tokyo.

I asked Mother to ask Grandmother to name the baby.

Two or three days later, I took my official seal and went into Tokyo to register the birth. I talked to Grandmother, who said she hadn't been able to come up with a good name – how would it be if we named it Rume after her? The second eldest of my sisters giggled and said it sounded funny. (It could have been that no one in her girls' school had a similar name.) I, however, liked Grandmother's name. Mother approved too.

Since it is said that trouble can result from two people having purely identical first and last names, we added the diminutive 'ko', making our daughter's name Rumeko.

XI

Now the time shifts to four weeks ago.

I saw a review of *Danshichi Kurobei* in the newspaper, and suddenly got the urge to go to the Kabuki theatre, something I hadn't done for quite a while.

M promised to accompany me to Tokyo on 23 August. *Danshichi*'s run would be over by then, but I had business that had to be taken care of that day. *Danshichi* might possibly be playing at another Kabuki theatre, but even if there weren't any good plays around, we could always take in the motion pictures instead. We agreed that I would run my errands first, then meet M on the second floor of Maruzen at twelve-thirty, or, if later, at the Takashimaya department store where his wife would be shopping.

The morning of the twenty-third, I left the house without pausing for breakfast to catch the first train to Tokyo. I got off at Minami-senjū to go see a friend on business at his home in Hashiba, spent an hour or so with him and then continued on to the Mitsui Bank in Nihonbashi. I intended my transaction there to take about fifteen minutes, but two hours passed with no real progress. As the clerks called out the numbers, I found myself expecting each one to be mine and so was helplessly pulled down into a state of utter frustration. Had I brought something to read, it might have been all right, but as it was, I could only sit planted on the bench, breathing in the unfamiliar air, feeling more and more on edge as my apprehension and disgust mounted. Every person around me was a complete stranger. I felt like oil dropped in water.

Finally, I couldn't stand it any longer and left without the money. It's a big building with a whole crowd of employees, I thought, but nobody's doing anything. To have been stuck on that bench so long and have nothing to show for it was horrible. Why, one could take the express to Kōzunosaki in that amount of time! And it was a rude place too, for not a soul had had the consideration to tell the faithful customer sitting there so unaware just how long he would have to wait.

Now I had to traverse the Nihonbashi Bridge to take care of a rather trivial matter at the Morimura Bank. As soon as I arrived, I filled out my forms, then crossed the street to a lacquerware shop to buy a set of stacked boxes for my wife. She needed these to hold the ceremonial red rice that we would serve after our visit to the shrine with the baby the next day. I phoned Azabu from the shop. Mother answered.

'Grandmother's dislocated her jaw,' she said.

That morning, according to Mother, Yoshiko had found Grandmother lying dazed in bed with her mouth hanging open. When Yoshiko spoke to her, she could only manage to nod and make a sort of 'aahing' sound. Grandmother had dislocated her jaw before (though I hadn't known about it) one evening while standing out on the veranda. Someone had exclaimed, 'Look, the moon is out!', she'd thrown her head back to see, and one side had popped out of joint. Remembering this, Yoshiko immediately called Mother. She phoned a physician relative of ours, but he turned out to be unwell. She then called another doctor, also a relative, but he was out of town. Mother had no choice but to phone the first doctor back to ask him to recommend someone else. Instead he took pity on them and, despite his own infirmity, came himself. One side of Grandmother's jaw had easily gone back into place, Mother told me, but the other side was difficult and painful.

'She's finally resting now, though she has a slight fever,' she said.

'How high is it?'

'38.3 when I took it a while ago.'

'That's pretty high,' I said. 'Look, there are just a couple of things I've got to take care of. Then I'll be over right away!'

'Well, all right,' Mother answered. Father must be home, I thought.

I hoisted the bulky parcel of boxes and left the shop. The Morimura Bank had already completed my transaction. I returned to the Mitsui Bank. They weren't ready yet.

I was worried about Grandmother. Today was the first I'd heard of her jaw dislocating. Though this alone presented no particular cause for alarm, I found it somehow saddening that her body had grown so fragile.

It was already a bit too late to catch M at Maruzen, so I went ahead to Takashimaya. Neither M nor his wife were anywhere in sight. Presently, however, they came climbing up the stairs together. They said they'd taken the next train.

The three of us ate lunch there. The news of Grandmother's illness had joined with my exasperation from the bank to put me in a thoroughly foul mood. When we finished our meal, M and I left the store. I didn't feel like going back to the bank yet. I figured if I waited until shortly before they closed at four o'clock, things might be settled more quickly, to say the least. After arranging to meet at a cinema in Asakusa at five o'clock, M and I parted, I heading for Azabu, M for Maruzen, where his wife would join him when she finished her shopping.

I felt physically and mentally exhausted. Lugging around that confounded parcel of lacquer boxes was making me feel even worse.

I got off the streetcar and rushed to the Azabu house. Dropping the parcel in the front hall, I went straight to Grandmother's room. Mother and Takako were there.

'Junkichi's come!' Mother said loudly, moving her face close to Grandmother's.

Grandmother's heavy eyelids opened slightly. I could see that her eyes were watery and bloodshot. Then they closed again.

I drew my face to hers.

'The baby's doing fine, Grandmother.'

She nodded imperceptibly but didn't open her eyes.

'A dislocated jaw is nothing to worry about,' I said, raising my voice a notch. Too weary even to nod, she made no response.

'Please fix her a pipe,' Mother said.

I filled the long narrow *kiseru* lying nearby with tobacco, lit it, and held it out for Grandmother. She relaxed her lips just enough to allow me to insert the stem in her mouth; then, with eyes still shut, she began to smoke. I doubted that she was fully conscious of what was going on.

A while later, Grandmother began to show signs of being bothered by something happening between her legs. Her bowels were starting to move. A chamber pot was brought in from the next room. After helping her up into a sitting position, I moved behind her, put my arms under her shoulders, and hoisted her over the pot until she could finish.

This was an awful blow for me. My chest ached. Grandmother was fastidious and stubborn to a fault, and her strong sense of propriety had always made her unwilling to relieve herself in her own room, even when seriously ill. I'd scolded her often on this score, but she had always claimed that 'it won't come out unless I'm in the toilet', and got to her feet on yet another pointless trip. Gradually, however, she'd stopped being so unreasonable. No longer did she mind having a chamber pot in her room. Even so, this was the first time to my knowledge that she had unwittingly soiled herself like this.

A maid brought some hot water and Mother set about gently cleansing Grandmother's lower parts. While this was going on, another maid came to the room. 'The master wishes to see you,' she said to Mother.

As soon as she finished tidying up, Mother got up and left.

Though Grandmother was eighty-two, her gaze was remarkably strong and full of life. I was aware she had grown much weaker over the past four or five years; yet, whenever I saw that look in her eye, I would relax and think 'not yet'. Her voice was surprisingly strong, too. Many was the time

I had seen her loudly ordering her maids and grandchildren about the house from where she sat. Hearing her shout like that always gave me a happy feeling. I had a real fear about her dying. Just the thought of Father and me clashing over her deathbed was too scary to contemplate. Even stronger than this fear, however, was my desire that she stay alive. In the story I mentioned earlier about the husband, the wife and the pregnant maid, I wrote that the wife's mother was critically ill, made her two years older than Grandmother and then had her recover in the end. I couldn't rest until I had somehow intervened with the fates on her behalf. But Grandmother's present condition put me at a loss as to where to fix my hopes. It was staggering to find out how easily her jaw had dislocated, and now I had witnessed her 'accident'. Wasn't that which I feared now coming to pass? I was terror-stricken.

Back came Mother, looking upset. She beckoned to me from the veranda. I got up and went out to her.

'Grandmother's out of danger now,' she said, 'so there's no more cause for worry. Why don't you call it a day and go home? Don't take this badly, please!' Although I was angry, I held my tongue. I couldn't fathom how she could say there was 'no cause for worry'.

'Nothing could be more undutiful to Grandmother,' she continued, 'than for you to quarrel with Father when she's sick like this.'

'As far as I'm concerned,' I said a bit heatedly, 'my relationship with Father and my relationship with Grandmother are two different things. Can't you see that?'

'Yes, I understand you perfectly.'

'Then let's make Father see it too. Whether he does or doesn't won't affect anything I do, but still I could put the matter to him calmly in a letter.'

'That would be fine. But remember, the calm must come from your heart.'

'Then maybe I should go talk to him now,' I said. 'Is he in his study?'

'Not now, please. Wait until you're nice and relaxed, then write to him.'

'I see. Well, all right, let's leave it at that. There's a favour I must ask you first though, Mother. Whenever you write you always try to describe Grandmother's health in a way that won't worry me. That only makes me more anxious. From now on, I want you to be honest – let me know how things really stand. If I feel you've left something out, I don't know how much to fill in and end up getting more worried!'

'You're right. I'll try to be more careful,' Mother said.

'Well, I'll leave now. But please cable me in Abiko tomorrow. I'll be back in two or three days either way, but send me a cable all the same, please!'

'I will. And remember, make your letter to Father as calm as possible – don't try to reason with him!' she reiterated.

Some five minutes later, I hoisted the bulky parcel of boxes once again and walked out of the Azabu house.

My mood was turning from bad to worse. I could picture Father enraged, his face purple, his veins bulging, commanding Mother, 'Send Junkichi home! Now!' I could actually hear his voice telling her, 'I don't want that fellow in this house – under any circumstances!'

I was exasperated. I was angry, too. Still, since nothing had happened that I hadn't expected, I was able to keep this exasperation from overwhelming me. This involved a conscious effort on my part, for Grandmother's condition was paining me deeply.

My wife had asked me to buy gifts for the people who'd sent congratulations on the birth of our baby. She wanted to have these sent off before we made our trip to the shrine the next day. Feeling physically and emotionally drained, I dragged myself off to Ginza to do the shopping. Soon, there were two more parcels to carry.

Shortly before four, I returned to the Mitsui Bank. At last my business there was brought to a close. Then I went on to Asakusa.

I rejoined M and his wife at the agreed-upon cinema. When one motion picture had ended, M showed me a large illustrated book of Rodin's sculpture that he'd bought at Maruzen that day. I'd barely had a chance to glance at three or four of the photographs when the theatre grew dark again. In my present mood, motion pictures didn't interest me in the least.

After about thirty minutes, the three of us left. We'd originally planned to continue on to another theatre, but no one mentioned that now. M and his wife were fitting their feelings to match mine. I found this wordless sharing of emotion among the three of us sustaining and comforting. Though they had their own parcels to carry, they took a portion of my load and divided it between them. When we stopped to eat, I telephoned Mother.

'Nothing much has changed, so don't worry,' came the reply.

The three of us left the restaurant a while later. As we strolled along the covered shopping arcade, I told M how I'd had to cut short my visit to Azabu. I was able to talk about it calmly.

'Your *père* is as stubborn as ever, isn't he?' M said, smiling a bit sadly.

Since we still had time before the last train to Abiko left at nine, we took the streetcar from Asakusa's Kaminari Gate past Ueno Station to Hironokōji, then walked back through the lively night streets.

We entered a shop in front of the station that sold sweetened shaved ice. I phoned Azabu again from there. I didn't like to keep making Mother come to the phone.

'Grandmother's still about the same, isn't she?' I asked the maid who answered.

'Yes, sir – there's been no change.'

'Well, all right then. Don't bother calling anyone,' I said and hung up.

I still felt completely drained. If my frame of mind doesn't improve, I thought, the whole mood of the 'Dreamer' piece I'm working on is liable to be shattered. I continued to feel dazed even after we were on the train.

About the time we pulled out of Kitasenjū, I began to leaf through M's book on Rodin. At first, I was too distracted to give it my full attention. Before long, though, the pictures began to suck me in. I became acutely aware of the eternal quality of Rodin's art. I could feel excitement bubbling up from the pit of my stomach, and with it a pleasurable sensation of liberation. It felt as if my own heart were flying off to seek Rodin's. This experience was strangely invigorating.

Sanzō and our dog Teru were waiting at Abiko Station together with someone from M's house. Teru kept trying to jump on me in her joy. When we reached the point where the road from the station forks in front of the shrine, I parted ways with M and his wife.

Running on ahead, straying off the road, then racing to catch up again, Teru happily followed us home, stopping here and there to pee along the way.

Sanzō told me that Y was supposed to be going into Tokyo early the next morning. As soon as I got home, I wrote a note asking him to phone Azabu to inquire after Grandmother for me before he came back. I sent Sanzō to deliver it without delay.

XII

The next day, I tried writing the letter to Father. Mother had merely stated the obvious when she warned me against reasoning with him logically. Could logic have done the trick, composing the letter would have been child's play. Yet, as I well knew, proving my request just and proper in that fashion would serve no real purpose. However cleverly I argued, however difficult I made it for him to justify barring me from the house, anything based on reason alone would only serve to worsen matters. I had no desire whatsoever to write such a letter. Instead, I tried composing something that would appeal to Father's emotions. I gave this up right away, though, for I found that such deliberate emotional manipulation called up feelings in me that were just too ugly to face.

After several attempts, I knew no letter could fully express my present feelings. The biggest problem was that my mental image of Father just wouldn't stand still. To put it another way, I found my feelings about him were constantly shifting. Each time I started writing, he would look calm, even conciliatory, and I could go ahead feeling quite calm myself. As I continued, however, Father's expression would gradually change, and I would respond by shifting from a factual to a more argumentative style. As soon as this happened, Father's face grew stubborn and cross, and I had no choice but to lay down my pen.

I felt I couldn't write to Father in my present state. I wrote a letter to Mother explaining that I had given up on the letter; I would go to Tokyo shortly instead and speak to Father in person.

A telegram came that afternoon.

> BETTER TODAY, TEMPERATURE 37.2, DOCTOR ISHIGURO CALLED, DIAGNOSIS INTESTINAL CATARRH, NURSE COMING, DONT WORRY.

As I had been afraid of the consequences should

Grandmother's condition remain unchanged for several days, this telegram put my mind at ease.

Around dinnertime, my friend from Hashiba stopped by to visit and continue our business of the day before. When he left to catch the final Tokyo-bound train scheduled at 10.12, I accompanied him as far as the station.

His train was a bit late, and the last train from Tokyo pulled in while we were waiting. Out stepped Y. Y had telephoned Azabu for me, and so was able to give a detailed report on Grandmother's condition. At this rate, I thought gratefully, my fears of yesterday will soon vanish into thin air. When the Tokyo-bound train pulled out, Y and I headed home together.

The next day, I saw in the paper that an old professor from Waseda University was ill, and in critical condition. Even though I rather disliked this old man, whose outstanding feature was an unusually large mouth, I now found myself hoping he would recover. Seasonal fluctuations in temperature can lead to a series of deaths among the aged: should this indeed be one of those times, Grandmother too might be affected – thus my sudden change of heart.

I resumed work on the 'Dreamer' piece, which I'd promised for the October issue of a certain journal.

I didn't hate Father now. I did worry, however, whether I could muster enough calm to keep my emotional equilibrium should Father vent his hatred of me to my face. When I had been living in Kyoto, I had received a letter from a cousin of mine attending prep school that contained the line, 'I hope the day will come when your father shall be enveloped in your vast love'. This had infuriated me at the time. 'People who have never experienced the true meaning of "vast love",' I wrote back, 'shouldn't recklessly throw the word at others!' Now, I recalled this incident. I was being a bit too conceited, I thought, to be so confident that I could keep my newfound harmony and composure in the face of whatever attitude Father might take. Unwittingly, I had committed the folly of acting as though I could 'envelop Father in my vast love', without being sure of the true strength of that love.

If I could retain my composure in the face of whatever attitude Father might take and then withdraw gracefully, without having been pushy or dishonest, that would be ideal. To expect this of my present self, however, involved a real leap of faith. There was a gap in the thinking somewhere.

At any rate, I could only wait until we met and see what happened. It would be sheer foolishness to think that events of the heart could somehow be predicted or arranged in advance.

30 August would mark the twenty-third anniversary of the death of my birth mother. If Father were at home when I went to Tokyo to visit her grave that day, I thought, I would go see him then.

XIII

On the thirtieth, I boarded the Tokyo-bound train with a bicycle under my arm. Our painter friend SK had ridden it out from the city two days before and then left it with us.

Arriving at Ueno, I got on the bicycle and pedalled off in the direction of Azabu.

I dismounted when I reached the foot of the hill that runs from Tanimachi up to the Azabu house. As I walked the bicycle up the slope, I pictured Father dressed in a man's kimono descending in my direction. This was not sheer fantasy. If Father's disgust at the prospect of meeting me had driven him from the house, he would surely choose this route, for it went in the opposite direction from the path to the closest streetcar stop. Should he pass this way, I decided, it would be best to speak to him. A picture of our meeting came to me. I stepped forward to say something, but he wordlessly tried to push past me and escape. I persisted in trying to talk and moved to block his way. In the end, however, he managed to get away, maintaining his silence until the end. I felt that this scenario, imagined though it was, came close to matching what would actually happen.

I arrived at the Azabu house. Inside the main entrance, I spied my Kamakura uncle's cane. I proceeded directly to Grandmother's quarters. Grandmother had that day ordered her bedding moved to another room right across the hall, and it was there that I found her, seated on some cushions. She looked much stronger than I'd expected. Even her powerful gaze had returned. I was overjoyed. Two nurses were in attendance, and my uncle, my sisters (who were dressed up in fancier kimonos than usual) and Mother were also in the room.

Grandmother wanted to know why I hadn't come earlier. She seemed disappointed that I had just missed the Buddhist priest's chanting of the sutras.

My uncle told me that he planned to visit Kyoto within the next two or three days.

'I had a dream last night that you were going to Kyoto to receive your priest's diploma,' said Grandmother. 'But then your mother was wondering if your type could still get one,' she smirked.

'My type can't get one?' said Uncle. 'That's a bit harsh. But it's true, we're still not eligible.'

'Uncle Masa,' asked Takako, 'are you going to get a diploma?'

'No, nothing like that,' laughed Uncle. 'That was only in Grandmother's dream. Uncle Masa's just going to see the old priest at Kenninji Temple for the first time in a long while. Come to think of it, perhaps I mentioned my plans to you. Somehow I doubt it, though.'

'I don't recall hearing anything,' Grandmother replied.

'Won't you come and light some incense for the Buddha?' asked Mother, who had been looking a little tense since my arrival.

I said yes and went out to the room that held our family shrine. Mother followed right behind me.

The shrine had been filled with offerings – lighted candles, incense, flowers, tea, cakes and fruit. On one side was hung a picture-scroll with the clumsily sewn portrait of my elder brother, dead at three, in the arms of our departed mother, the 'Buddha', whose spirit was being welcomed that day.

I lit a stick of incense and bowed before the shrine.

'Father's home, isn't he?' I asked Mother, who had seated herself beside me.

'Yes, he's in.'

'I just couldn't express the way I felt in a letter, so I thought it best to come meet him face-to-face.'

'Well, if you can really stay calm when you talk to him, nothing could be better, but I implore you, calm yourself first and then speak quietly. Since this morning I've visited this shrine many times to beg your mother's spirit for guidance. Please don't let your feelings of the moment lead you to speak in anger – just a word of apology is enough. Grit your teeth and tell him – I was wrong and I'm sorry. Your father's getting on in years, and he suffers terribly because of his relationship with you. That's why if you could manage just a word of apology he'd be completely satisfied. He's not the sort who gives in easily either, you know, and now he feels that as a parent he can't be the one to break the ice – that's not too unreasonable, is it? Stubborn, oh yes, your father's very stubborn, but he's not really bad you know,' Mother pleaded, her eyes full of tears.

'Yes, that's true,' I answered. 'But I see things another way. What's happened between Father and me up till now has been unavoidable. To have acted any other way would have spelled real trouble for me. I know this has been hard on Father. I know I've sometimes been in the wrong. But I did what I had to and I have no regrets. Suppose I'd become the kind of person Father would have liked – judged by my eyes today, that person would be worthless.'

'Yes, I understand, I'm perfectly aware that people who think it's enough to meekly assent to whatever their parents say aren't worth much. But that doesn't mean you'd suddenly lose the ability to stand on your own two feet if you went to your father and said a word of apology. Please, I beseech you, tell him how sorry you are, that it was all your fault. If you could just manage that, then Father and Grandmother and then the whole household would brighten up and we could all live together happily. Just swallow your pride and apologise! Please, I implore you!' Mother's head kept bowing in excitement as she spoke.

'But I can't swallow my pride and apologise if

that's not how I feel. Don't you see, what you're asking me to do is try to cross a broad moat in one leap. Even if I succeeded for the moment, sooner or later Father would come to realise that the moat separating us was still there, at which point my apology would have been useless, even if it was formally correct.'

I went on.

'At any rate, I'll go give it a try. I can't prepare anyway, since emotions are involved and they can't be planned ahead. Who knows, maybe I'll feel calmer than I expect.'

'That's right. If you're calm, everything is sure to go smoothly.'

'Is Father in his study?'

'I think so. If not, try the inner room.'

I got up and headed for Father's Western-style room. I could feel my heart quaking with apprehension. It's no good going in there like this, I thought. I paced back and forth in the tatami hallway trying to calm myself. I didn't think at all about how I would go about broaching the conversation with Father. Within two minutes or so my emotions had quieted down. I went to the door of the study and knocked.

No answer. I opened the door and looked inside. Father wasn't there. I went back to Grandmother's room.

'He's not there,' I told Mother.

'He may be in the garden,' she said, getting to her feet. 'I'll go call him.'

A moment later she came hurrying back.

'The study,' she said.

The study door was open. I could see Father sitting in the chair in front of his desk, which he had turned around to face the door. His expression was calm.

'Pull up a seat,' he said, nodding towards the chairs lined up beneath the window and pointing at the floor before me. I placed a chair there and sat down facing him. I remained silent.

'Let's hear what you've got to say first,' Father said. 'Is Masa out there?' he went on. The way he spoke gave me a good impression.

'Yes, he is,' I replied.

Father rose and rang the bell on the wall, then sat back down.

'Well?' he said, trying to draw me out of my silence.

A maid came to see what he wanted.

'Ah, yes. Ask my wife's brother to come here,' Father said.

'I think it's senseless for you and me to go on the way we are,' I began.

'Uh-huh.'

'Up until now there's been no way around it. I know it's been hard on you. Sometimes, I think I've acted badly too.'

'Uh-huh,' Father nodded. I was so agitated that it sounded as if I were overcome with anger. This was altogether different from the 'calm and quiet' tone I'd been promising Mother all along. Looking back now, however, I feel nothing could have been more fitting for Father and me at that moment; it was natural for me to speak that way under the circumstances.

'What's done is done. It just seems ridiculous to let things go on like this.'

My uncle entered. He sat down in a chair behind me.

'All right,' Father said. 'But then what? Is this change to last just until Grandmother recovers, or do you mean to make it more permanent?'

'Until meeting you now, Father, I never expected it could be permanent,' I said. 'I would have been happy just to receive your permission to visit Grandmother freely until she gets well. In my heart of hearts, though, I want it to be more than that.' My eyes were brimming with tears, but I held on.

'I see,' said Father. He was close to tears himself, and his lips were pressed tightly together. 'To tell you the truth,' he said after a moment, 'I'm getting on in years, and the thought that our relationship would go on this way has pained me deeply. There were times I was sure I hated you. Ever since you vowed to leave the family several years ago, you've turned a deaf ear to my every attempt to speak to you. I've been at a total loss. I never intended to throw you out – I let you go because I had no choice. That's how it's been until today . . .'

As he said this, Father began to cry. I was crying as well. Behind me, my uncle started to say something, then he too broke into loud sobs.

After a while, Father stood up and rang the bell on the wall.

'Call my wife immediately,' he told the maid who came.

Mother entered. She sat down on a low chair beside Father.

'Junkichi says he thinks things have been really bad up to now too. He wants us to return to live as father and son again for now and the future . . . that's right, isn't it?' He broke off, turning to me.

'Yes,' I nodded. When Mother saw this, she rushed to where I was sitting and clasped my hands tight in hers.

'Thank you, Junkichi, thank you,' she said through her tears, lowering her head repeatedly to my chest. I felt I had to bow back, but when I tried her head came up and her bun of hair struck me in the mouth.

'Masa, thank you, thank you,' she poured out her heartfelt thanks to her brother.

'Go tell Grandmother,' Father said. Mother hurried out, wiping the tears from her face.

All four of my sisters, right down to six-year-old Rokuko, came in. Instead of joining us, they hung together, bowing as a group.

'Let's go over to Abiko tomorrow,' Father said suddenly when everyone had gone. He looked at me as though to ask if it were convenient.

'We'd love to have you.'

'Good. I want to see Rumeko and find out what kind of a house you're living in,' Father said brightly.

'By all means,' I said.

XIV

Grandmother's bedding had been returned to her own room at some point during my absence. I was there talking with her, Uncle, and the rest of the family when Father came in.

'Have you been told about Junkichi?' he asked Grandmother.

'Yes,' she nodded.

Father seemed to be waiting for her to go on. Why can't she try a little harder to respond to his feelings, I thought critically. But then again it was Grandmother's nature not to show any emotion. Father started to say something more, but then fell silent. He seemed moved in some way, for he kept glancing over towards the family shrine, where the clumsy portrait of my dead mother and brother that I mentioned before was hung.

Father drank sake with his lunch. Mother, my uncle, my sisters and I all had one cup each. Those who didn't drink pretended to.

No one asked what it was we were celebrating. We could feel a gentle elation flowing among our hearts linking them together, but no one spoke of it. It was a good feeling. We chatted on about this and that. Suddenly Father remembered something.

'Okō!' he ordered the maid, 'Telegraph Fusako and tell her about today!' Fusako was the eldest of my sisters who lived in Kamakura.

'Why don't I go tell her in person?' suggested my uncle. 'If not tonight then early tomorrow.'

'Well now, what a fine idea,' Father replied. 'So who's going to Abiko tomorrow?' he went on, glancing significantly at my little sisters.

'Rokuko's going!'

'Masako's going too!'

'Good,' said Father with a smile. 'How about the big girls?'

'We're all going,' said Yoshiko.

Although I'd eaten scarcely any breakfast, I had no appetite for lunch at all. I just mixed a little of the wine Father had ordered with water and sipped on that.

After lunch, we went to Aoyama Cemetery. Father, who'd had a bit too much to drink, had decided to take a bath to sober up before going, and Grandmother was staying behind, so altogether there were seven in our party. I took the bicycle, which I rode when they were on the streetcar; the rest of the time I walked alongside my uncle. Neither of us brought up what had happened that day. Mother too said nothing.

After paying a visit to my baby's grave, I bid everyone farewell and bicycled to SK's place in Yotsuya.

I found SK watering his garden. While he was finishing up and washing his feet, I was able to write Mother a letter of thanks. In it, I thanked her for never having abandoned hope of a reconciliation between Father and me, despite the countless failures and the excruciating role she had had to play for so long. I told her among other things that I hadn't had to leap across the moat – instead, I had unexpectedly found myself standing on the other side, as relaxed and calm as could be.

I felt sure, I wrote, that our reconciliation would last.

I described the day's events to SK. He was very happy for me, and I basked in the warmth of his friendship.

'Why don't you send a telegram to Sadako,' he suggested. 'I bet she'll be overjoyed to hear the news.'

'I don't think she knew I was going to see Father,' I replied, 'so I doubt she's particularly worried.'

A while later, two more friends dropped by as arranged.

I'd started to feel physically and emotionally exhausted the moment I arrived at SK's. It was not a disagreeable sensation. Like a small mountain lake enfolded in thick mist, my exhaustion carried with it the slightly dizzying sensation of absolute quiet. It was akin to the weariness of a traveller who has just returned home from a very long and trying journey.

Giving myself enough time to catch the last train to Abiko, I said my goodbyes and set off for Ueno.

Sanzō met me at the Abiko station, lantern in hand.

'We heard the master from Azabu is coming tomorrow,' he said as he followed me home.

'Did a telegram come?'

'At about three this afternoon.'

'The children will be coming too, so if the weather's good we can take them clam-digging. Please bring the boat around to the front of the house in the morning.'

'Certainly, sir. I've already been to the poultry shop to order the chicken for tomorrow's meal.'

'I see. Well, come a little early if you can to help tidy up a bit around the house.'

'It's already done. Your wife helped us clean everything, inside and out.'

When I turned up the slope to my home, I could see my wife waiting for me. She came down and squeezed my hands in hers.

'Congratulations,' she said.

XV

The following morning, I went to the station to greet our guests by myself. Although my wife wanted to join me, the baby seemed oddly jumpy, so I made her stay at home.

The train pulled in. The first to get off was Takako, followed by Rokuko and Masako. Then Father stepped down. I bowed to him.

'Hello,' he responded with a light nod, his face devoid of expression.

When we left the station, I still hadn't really spoken to Father. We were both feeling inhibited with each other. I expected this inhibition would fade before long. What we should not do, I thought, was to try and break the ice by forcing a conversation. Father too refrained from unnecessary talk.

We all boarded rickshaws for the ride to my

home. My wife came through the front gate to meet us, baby in arms. She started to cry when she saw Father. Father's eyes were on the baby.

I felt good all that day. Our inhibitions quickly vanished, and we spent most of our time discussing things like ceramics and paintings. I pulled out my meagre collection of antique pottery and fabrics to show Father. He talked about some hanging scrolls he'd bought recently. We weren't bored at all. Nothing was said about the events of the previous day. When the children had gone outside to play, however, Father did speak to my wife.

'Junkichi says he wishes to re-establish our relationship as father and son on a permanent basis, something which is my hope as well. I want you to join with us to make it as though the past had never happened.'

Dabbing at her eyes, my wife silently nodded her assent. Father looked as though he were going to continue in this vein, and I guessed that he might be about to repeat what he had told Mother the previous day. Even if he went through all that again, though, I felt confident I could handle it without getting upset. Father, however, dropped the subject. This struck me very favourably. I was grateful to him.

'Whatever happened to little Satoko?' Father said. We couldn't answer. I realised then, however, that I no longer bore him any ill feeling for her death.

It was decided that everyone would go back on the three p.m. train.

'From now on, I'll be coming to see you every so often,' Father said to my wife when he left.

'Please do come again.'

'Please do,' I chimed in.

I took them to the station. Their train was late.

'I'll be too busy to come to Tokyo for a while,' I told Yoshiko. Little Masako overheard me.

'But you will come this year, won't you?' she cried, looking up at me. 'For sure, right? It'll all be fine. For sure.'

My sisters all laughed. Some idea seemed to have taken hold of Masako, though, for she kept repeating herself over and over. There was no doubt that even in the heart of this little girl, not yet eight years old, the reconciliation was far from a small event.

Father was looking a bit tired. Soon the train

arrived. Everybody climbed aboard. Father took a window seat on the far side of the car. My sisters all piled in on the platform side and pressed their faces in a row against the window.

When the whistle blew, they all said their farewells. As I stood there, cap in hand, I noticed Father was looking my way, so I gave a parting bow.

He murmured a brief goodbye and nodded back. This vague response somehow struck me as unsatisfying. I cast him a strange look, something between a frown and a look of sadness. Then suddenly a certain expression came into his eyes. This expression was what I had been seeking, although I hadn't known it until then. As our two hearts met and touched, I could feel happiness and excitement contort my face even further. The train began to pull out. My sisters waved and waved as if they would never stop. When the train had passed the long platform and was bending out of sight off to the right, they were still waving. An eternity later, I found myself standing there alone on the platform under my umbrella. I left the station and rushed home. I didn't understand why I was in such a hurry. There can be no more doubt, I thought.

Father and I are truly reconciled. There was love for him in my heart, and I could sense it melting away all the bad feelings from our past.

XVI

I had lost all desire to continue work on the 'Dreamer' piece that dealt with my troubles with Father. I had no choice but to look for something else to write about. Actually, I did have some material, but it would take time to really get my heart into whatever I chose. Some things, I felt, might never involve me deeply again. If I forced myself to write about them, bloodless works would result. These would be failures. Could I produce a story that would amount to something by the promised date of 15 or 16 September?

Even as I pondered this problem, my mind kept slipping back to savour my reconciliation with Father. I wanted to see him again very soon. I felt that at this juncture it made sense to see him right away rather than wait two or three more weeks.

Then I hit on an idea – to show Father how I felt, I would use some of the money I had earned to commission SK to paint his portrait, which I could then present to him as a gesture of my affection. I felt that asking SK, who had shared in the joy of the reconciliation, counted for something too. I wrote a letter to SK on the spot.

After posting the letter the next morning (2 September), I decided it would actually be better to start the ball rolling by going right into Tokyo to see Father and SK in person.

On my way to the train station, I stopped by the post office to pick up my mail. There was a letter from my sister in Kamakura. I read it as I walked along.

'Uncle Masa stopped by early this morning when I was still in bed to tell us the happy, happy news. I cried when I heard.'

She had addressed the letter to both me and my wife. I wept.

When I arrived at Ueno, I made my way directly to the Azabu house. I headed for Father's study as soon as I got there but he wasn't in.

'Then I bet he's in the garden,' said little Masako, who had followed me in from the front entrance. ‘Father! Father!’ she called loudly from the veranda of the tatami-floored drawing room.

Father came rushing out of the garden pavilion. He seemed to be under the impression that he was wanted on the phone.

I slipped on the garden clogs and stepped down into the garden.

The inhibitions we’d experienced that morning in Abiko two days before still remained, making us a bit stiff with each other. I accepted this as inevitable. I mentioned the portrait and asked whether or not he would mind sitting for it. He consented happily.

I left Father standing pensively there in the garden and headed back into the house. Just when I reached the veranda, however, he suddenly turned towards me as if to speak. I returned a step, whereupon he broke off whatever he was about to say and looked down at his feet. Then he walked off.

On my way to see Grandmother, I stopped by Mother’s room. She was ill and in bed. She said that she had been told it was her large intestine that was causing her trouble – persistent diarrhoea and lack of appetite that had left her completely exhausted.

'Maybe it's because I'm emotionally worn out,' she said, 'and now that things are finally settled I can let go a bit.'

'Is that so. Did Yoshiko tell you about what happened the day before yesterday?'

'Yes. I received a letter from Sadako, too. I'm really not worried at all any more.'

I stayed with her a little longer before going to visit Grandmother. She looked very well. Her bedding was still laid out, but she was seated on a cushion in another part of the room.

'I think this time things are going to be all right,' I told her. 'No one's forcing their feelings at all.'

'Aah, that's really wonderful,' she replied, her face glowing with an aura of deep well-being that had been absent three days before. 'When my sister Otaka went back home, our whole family gathered to hear the news. She said that they all cried. There, it's all in those letters,' Grandmother said, gesturing at several envelopes piled on her bed.

'You don't say,' I replied, ignoring the letters.

Grandmother went on to describe how Father had praised Abiko as being 'better than he expected', how he had admired the house and garden, and so on. Presently she fell silent.

While I blithely kept on chatting about this and that, Grandmother sat there impassively, her face turned towards the floor. She must have thought of something that moves her, I thought. At the same time, I was a bit worried her jaw might have popped out again, though her lips were pressed tightly shut.

When a maid came in and said something, Grandmother answered her readily.

My sister from Kamakura arrived with her baby.

Father showed up a little while later.

'It's too bad Masa couldn't come,' he said, 'but since we're all gathered here today, let's go out to eat.'

We decided to eat at the Sannōdai Restaurant. I made the reservations, fixing the time at four p.m. so I could catch my train back to Abiko.

Shortly thereafter, I left the Azabu house and went to SK's. He had gone to Nagatachō to play tennis. I headed there myself and arrived to find SK drenched in sweat playing a singles match with H. Thirty minutes later we left the courts together. SK said he had two projects that he had agreed to finish by a certain date in October. He could start work on Father's portrait then, if it was all right with me. I said it was.

H and I went along to SK's house. At about two o'clock, I left them there and headed back to Azabu. My Kamakura sister's husband came moments after I arrived.

That made eight of us in all, but my younger brother Junzō still hadn't returned, and Father was growing worried. He even ordered that all likely places be telephoned.

Finally we could wait no more. Since it was drizzling outside, the women took rickshaws. Father, my sister's husband and I walked.

We arrived at the restaurant and still Junzō hadn't shown up. Father was so anxious it was funny.

'It really bothers me when people don't come on time,' he said as if trying to justify himself.

Even so, Father was in good humour. It was only natural that, playing the role of host as he was, Junzō's failure to come at the promised time with everyone waiting and the food prepared would tax his patience. Junzō had better show up before Father gets too upset, I thought. Although his worry was obvious, however, Father didn't grow angry. I felt he was curbing his exasperation so as not to disrupt the peaceful tenor of the day. I sensed too, however, that a new harmony was likely stirring within his breast, quelling his anger.

'Let's try waiting a bit more,' Father said to me, 'and then I guess we'll have to start.'

One day, three and a half years before, Father had done something which had infuriated me. Father apparently wasn't aware how angry I was, though, for the following day he had suddenly proposed to take us all out to eat at this very restaurant. He had made the reservations, specifying the number of people and so on. I decided I was in no mood to go along, however, and had told Mother as much before heading out by myself for the day around noontime.

'Why didn't Junkichi come?' Grandmother told me Father kept saying at the restaurant. Now I recalled that incident. Then, I had had no choice but to do what I did. Now, though, I felt fresh pity for Father over the grief that I had caused him.

Just after we started eating, Junzō arrived and Father grew altogether cheerful.

It was about seven o'clock when we left the restaurant. I still had two hours remaining before the last train.

Father said he was heading home, as the drink had made him rather sleepy, but that we could see him off by joining him for a stroll towards the Ginza.

When we reached Tameike, Father boarded a rickshaw for the remainder of his journey.

I looked into his eyes when we said goodbye. Our day together had filled them with a natural radiance, the glow of a love that was at once free and lighthearted. Never again would I doubt the stability of our reconciliation.

I bid farewell to everyone at the Ginza.

Day by day, the time left to finish my piece slipped away. I was beginning to grow concerned. I decided to write about that which was most on my mind – the reconciliation.

Half a month passed. I received a letter from my uncle, who had returned to Kamakura from Kyoto. It was written in response to my letter of thanks that I'd sent him at the beginning of the month.

'Your reconciliation with your father, I am convinced, was truly meant to be. He has told me that he thinks all will be well from now on. When I read in your letter that you are sure it is not a passing thing, my last doubt was swept away. I am reminded of the lines from an old Chinese poem:

From East and West, South and North
We make our way home at last
Together in the depths of night
We look out upon the same snow-capped peaks.'